*Maybe he was just a damn fool,*
*Clint decided.*

A fool for Savannah Heller. Who had dumped him. Deserted him. And not even let him know why.

Only a fool would go after a woman who had done that to him once already.

But Clint couldn't help himself. Couldn't stop wanting her.

What they'd had before should have lasted a lifetime.

And, foolish or not, Clint knew deep down that he was going to ask Savannah questions. That he was going to try to right whatever had gone wrong fifteen years ago. That he was going to give it a second chance.

And if he got hurt again?

It was a risk he had to take.

Because Savannah Heller was under his skin. And back in town…

Dear Reader,

Spring is in the air! It's the perfect time to pick wildflowers, frolic outdoors…and fall in love. And this March, Special Edition has an array of love stories that set the stage for romance!

Bestselling author Victoria Pade delivers an extra-special THAT SPECIAL WOMAN! title. The latest installment in her popular A RANCHING FAMILY series, *Cowboy's Love* is about a heroine who passionately reunites with the rugged rancher she left behind. Don't miss this warm and wonderful tale about love lost—and found again.

Romantic adventure is back in full force this month when the MONTANA MAVERICKS: RETURN TO WHITEHORN series continues with *Wife Most Wanted* by Joan Elliott Pickart—a spirited saga about a wanted woman who unwittingly falls for the town's sexiest lawman! And don't miss *Marriage by Necessity,* the second book in Christine Rimmer's engaging CONVENIENTLY YOURS miniseries.

Helen R. Myers brings us *Beloved Mercenary,* a poignant story about a gruff, brooding hero who finds new purpose when a precious little girl—and her beautiful mother—transform his life. And a jaded businessman gets much more than he bargained for when he conveniently marries his devoted assistant in *Texan's Bride* by Gail Link. Finally this month, to set an example for his shy teenage son, a confirmed loner enters into a "safe" relationship with a pretty stranger in *The Rancher Meets His Match* by Patricia McLinn.

I hope you enjoy this book, and each and every story to come!

Sincerely,

Tara Gavin
Senior Editor and Editorial Coordinator

Please address questions and book requests to:
Silhouette Reader Service
U.S.: 3010 Walden Ave., P.O. Box 1325, Buffalo, NY 14269
Canadian: P.O. Box 609, Fort Erie, Ont. L2A 5X3

# VICTORIA PADE

## COWBOY'S LOVE

SPECIAL EDITION®

Published by Silhouette Books

America's Publisher of Contemporary Romance

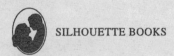

SILHOUETTE BOOKS

ISBN 0-373-24159-3

COWBOY'S LOVE

**Printed in U.S.A.**

**Books by Victoria Pade**

Silhouette Special Edition

\*A Ranching Family

---

# VICTORIA PADE

is a bestselling author of both historical and contemporary romance fiction, and mother of two energetic daughters, Cori and Erin. Although she enjoys her chosen career as a novelist, she occasionally laments that she has never traveled farther from her Colorado home than Disneyland, instead spending all her spare time plugging away at her computer. She takes breaks from writing by indulging in her favorite hobby—eating chocolate.

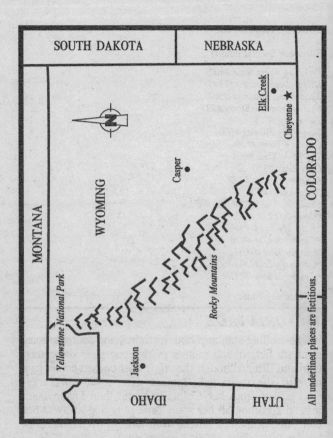

All underlined places are fictitious.

## Chapter One

"Hey, pretty lady! Come on out here and give me a big wet one right on the mouth!"

Savannah Heller was in the upstairs bedroom she'd shared with her younger sister in the house in which they'd grown up. Standing in front of the mirror that hung over the bureau, she was dressed only in her bathrobe, her bare feet curled away from the chill of the hard, wooden floor on this October morning. She was towel drying her hair, but at the sound of the male voice calling from out back she stopped short.

Not that the man was calling to her. He wasn't. It was Cully Culhane, yelling for her sister, Ivey.

But it didn't matter. Savannah's pulse still began to race. Her skin felt flushed. A wave of something that felt suspiciously like excitement washed through her.

Because she knew her sister's fiancé wasn't alone. And all she could think was, *Clint is here....*

Clint Culhane. Cully's brother.

She'd known Clint was coming over this morning with Cully. Ivey had warned her. So the sound of Cully calling to Ivey was an announcement to Savannah that Clint had arrived, too. And that was all it took to erupt a world of emotions in her.

Good and bad.

Trying to ignore them, she forced herself to go on drying her hair, staring straight ahead as if she were concentrating on the pendulum swing of a hypnotist's watch, trying not to give in to the urge to go to the window and look out at Clint.

Nothing less than the death of her best friend's husband could have brought Savannah back to Elk Creek, Wyoming, the small town where she'd been raised. Not that she had anything against Elk Creek. It was a fine place. Her reasons for staying away had more to do with Clint Culhane. Her first love. The man she'd left behind fifteen years ago. Lock, stock, barrel, bags and a secret she'd carried with her all this time. A secret that still shadowed her. And would, she had no doubt, for the rest of her life.

But when Della Dennehy's husband, Bucky, had died suddenly of a heart attack, Savannah had had to come back for the funeral and for whatever she could do for Della. Back to the small town. Back to the old house and all the memories. Back to where Clint was. The man she'd kept that secret from.

It hadn't been easy seeing Clint at the service or afterward at Della's house, but at least there'd been enough people around for Savannah to avoid any contact with him. Which was exactly what she'd done. But she knew she couldn't do that forever. Certainly not when he and his brother came to tend to things in the barn they rented. It was on the small farm Savannah and Ivey had inherited but hadn't used since leaving home. The barn that was only a few yards from the house...where he was now.

Her straight, very, very strawberry blond hair was dry by then so she set aside the towel and again put some effort into staying where she was, rather than heading for the window that faced the barn.

Maintaining her focus on her own reflection in the mirror, she brushed the tangles from her hair. But as she trained her attention on that reflection, she started wondering what Clint saw when he looked at her. Had she changed much in fifteen years?

Some, she decided. But maybe not a lot. Certainly not so much that anyone in Elk Creek wouldn't recognize her.

Sure, her hair was long now—five or six inches below her shoulders—a great deal longer than it ever was when she'd been under the heavy hand of her father, who had demanded that it be kept chopped off. But other than that, her face was about the same. More mature, lacking the strain that life with Silas Heller had put there, but about the same.

She still had a smattering of freckles across a nose that turned up just a little at the tip. She still had high, apple-round cheekbones that helped balance out the chin and jaw her father had always said were stubborn. Her forehead was slightly higher than she would like it to be, but she couldn't be bothered with bangs to camouflage it. There weren't any lines around lips that were a bit full, or around her eyes, either—unless she smiled and then just the hint of a crease or two showed up at the corners.

She could still get by without wearing much makeup or fussing over herself, which was good, because Savannah wasn't a fussy kind of person. Her sister, Ivey, said there was a lot of the tomboy left in her from their childhood, and Savannah supposed that was true, because she was more comfortable in a pair of blue jeans and a sweater than she ever was in dresses.

But what did Clint see when he looked at her? she kept wondering. Did he see that the woman in her had blossomed? Did he notice that her body had more curves than it had so long ago? That her skin was smoother, clearer? That longer hair helped fill out a bone structure that could almost seem gaunt otherwise?

Or maybe what she was really wondering was, did he *like* what he saw….

Not that it mattered. No reason it should. After all, they were just old acquaintances, she told herself. In fact, he might not even remember enough about her to compare the old Savannah with the new.

Yet it did matter what he thought, another part of her admitted reluctantly. And if he liked what he saw.

It mattered a whole lot….

"Are we going to work today or are you just plannin' to play kissy-face?"

That voice came from outside, too. But it wasn't Cully's voice. Those were the deep bass tones of Clint. He'd had that low voice by the time they'd graduated high school and Savannah would have recognized it anywhere—by the sound of it and by the chord it strummed inside her.

Even after all these years.

And as if it was an irresistible lure—or maybe the straw that broke the camel's back of her will-power—she suddenly found herself helpless to resist drifting toward that window. She walked between the two narrow beds that had been hers and Ivey's as kids and stopped at the small table between them that acted as a nightstand. Almost involuntarily she looked down at the barn. At the man who was stacking hay for the coming winter alongside it.

He was dressed for work in dusty old cowboy boots, a chambray shirt with the sleeves rolled to his elbows and a pair of blue jeans that were worn nearly white in places.

The jeans weren't so tight that they inhibited him as he wielded hooks to clasp on to the hay bales and hoist them from the rear of the truck to carry them to the barnside. But they also didn't hide the fact that he had long legs, with thighs thick enough to test the fabric, and a rear end to die for.

His narrow waist was encircled with a hand-tooled belt and held together with a none-too-small silver buckle that reflected the early-morning sunshine when he reared back to take the weight of the bales onto himself. From the flat belly behind the buckle, his torso widened in a sharp V where broad, work-honed shoulders filled out his shirt and flexed with the strain of the chore.

He'd left his hat on a corner post of the rail fence that surrounded the paddock, so his shiny chestnut hair was exposed. It was short on the sides, slightly longer on top and so thick and coarse—with just a hint of wave—that the top partly stood up and partly curved back, all haphazardly, as if it benefited from a finger raking more often than a comb.

Still he didn't look messy or unkempt. His hair somehow worked and seemed just right for him— carelessly neat, lacking any kind of vanity.

His sideburns were just a tad long, too, adding a rakish sexiness to a face she couldn't see clearly at that distance. She'd first noticed the sideburns when she'd peeked at him at the funeral. She'd noticed his sexiness, too. Inappropriate as that had been.

"Man! Do I have to hose you two off?" he called just then to his brother.

Savannah didn't know about Ivey and Cully, but a good dousing might help her, because the longer she looked down at Clint, the warmer she felt.

He was a big man. Bigger than he'd been when she'd left. Then he'd had the body of not much more than a wiry teenage boy. But now he was a pillar of solid muscle that looked powerful enough to make him a force to be reckoned with.

He was still light on his feet, though, she thought, remembering a summer's night long ago when he'd played his truck radio until the battery was nearly dead so they could dance out under the stars in the open countryside. She'd been surprised by how grace-ful he was and that grace was there even now in the symphony of movements of his body, which had turned from a boy's into a man's without her being there to see it.

She regretted missing out on that evolution.

But more, she had to fight the desire to get to know the newer version....

Oh, no, being back in Elk Creek was not going to be easy.

Savannah had a sudden rush of panic that made her want to leave town right away before that warmth, before those desires, got any worse. Any more difficult to resist.

But she couldn't leave.

Della needed her support. Ivey needed help with wedding plans and wanted her to act as maid of honor in the ceremony that would join Ivey and Cully as man and wife. Not even work was an excuse to go back to Cheyenne where she and Ivey had been living since leaving Elk Creek, because she was on sabbatical from the junior high school where she taught eighth-grade English composition.

There was just no way out. She had to stay.

And staying meant not only seeing Clint from afar, but being in the same room with him when his family and hers mixed and mingled for wedding events. It meant seeing him close up. Having to talk to him. Having to act as if those fifteen years had wiped away all they'd shared before.

But had they?

She wished he was nothing more than a faint memory to her. Everything would be so much simpler if that were the case.

But he wasn't.

On the other hand, maybe that was all she was for him.

Why did she hate that possibility so much? She

should be hoping that was the case. Hoping he barely remembered her.

But she wasn't hoping that. She couldn't. No matter how hard she tried.

"Ivey has fresh coffee and cinnamon rolls waitin' in the kitchen. Let's have a little before we do the hay," Cully called to Clint outside.

Savannah watched as Clint shook his head and seemed to laugh to himself. Then he made some remark she couldn't hear as he took off the leather work gloves that covered his hands, tossed them into the truck bed and headed for the house.

That was as much as it took for Savannah's heart to start beating triple time.

She stood perfectly still, listening to the sound of Clint, Cully and Ivey coming in. The old screen door of the mudroom creaked and then slammed shut after them. Laughter and joking voices rose up through the floorboards.

And all Savannah could think was that now Clint wasn't even a barnyard away.

He was just downstairs....

Suddenly her worries about being in the same room with him turned into a terrible yearning, and she couldn't help thinking that she had only to descend some stairs, turn a corner and cross the living room and dining room to be with him.

Into her mind's eye popped an image of herself doing just that, of finally coming face-to-face with Clint without a sea of other faces between them, of her gaze meeting his directly.

She wondered if—since they wouldn't be in a social setting—his expression would light up the way it used to when they were alone. Would he smile? Would he let his eyes run the length of her to see the changes? Would he find what he saw appealing?

And without a lot of people around, might he even come to her and give her just a friendly hug? A hug that would wrap her in those arms that had felt so good that she could still close her eyes and relive the sensations? Would he pull her close to that big, hard body and let her drink in the clean scent his hair had always had? Would he kiss her cheek? Or maybe more than her cheek?...

"Oh my gosh," she whispered, when she realized what she was thinking, yanking hard on those thoughts to bring them back into reality.

What had gotten into her? This was so unlike her. She was always levelheaded. Rational. Responsible. She was the voice of reason in any chaotic situation, the anchor that brought other people down to earth. She was pragmatic. Practical. She didn't get carried away by emotion or romantic notions or flights of fancy.

How could she be standing there, straining to hear a man's voice, letting herself be agitated over just the thought of being in a room with him? How could she be daydreaming—worse yet, *fantasizing* about it?

There was no basis for any of what was going on in her mind, in her body, she told herself firmly. What had gone on between her and Clint had occurred when they were just ending their teens. Barely more than kids, that's all they'd been. And fifteen *years* had passed since then. Their relationship was history, plain and simple, and it was ridiculous to fret over any of this, let alone imagine some kind of tender reunion.

She straightened her shoulders and marched away from the window, back to the bureau, pointed a stern index finger at her reflection in the mirror above it and said, "You'll see him. You'll talk to him. It won't be any different from any meaningless meeting with any other man."

And she would try not to think about the past when she met him again, because the past was over and done with. It couldn't be changed. It couldn't be relived. It didn't have any bearing on the present.

And she would get through this.

In fact, it suddenly occurred to her that maybe she should go downstairs right then and jump the first hurdle of actually speaking to him. At least she'd be on her own turf, without a lot of onlookers around.

The more she considered that, the wiser it seemed.

Or maybe it seemed wise because it was what she really wanted to do.

But one way or another she was tired of analyzing it all. Certainly there was no harm in going downstairs.

But she couldn't do it in her bathrobe.

Moving away from the bureau, she took that off, flung it onto the bed and dug through her unpacked suitcase until she found what she was looking for—a pair of leggings and an oversize Henley tunic. Casual clothes she'd wear around the house on any lazy Saturday when she wasn't anticipating company. Nothing special.

Then she went to the dresser again, where Ivey had makeup set out, and put on a little mascara before she could argue the point that she ordinarily wore it only for special occasions.

A few quick swipes of a comb through her hair, a bit of lip gloss, and she deemed herself ready.

Or at least as ready as she was ever going to be.

She took a deep breath, sighed it out and, like a drill sergeant giving a new recruit an order, said, ''Be cool. The two of you are only former friends.''

Well, more than friends. But former, anyway.

Then she made herself leave the bedroom at a slower pace than her legs were trying for, wishing she could decrease the speed of her pulse the same way.

But there was nothing she could do about that. It raced like crazy in spite of the fact that she did a leisurely wandering down the stairs as if she didn't have a clue that anyone else was in the house.

At the foot of the steps she turned to her right. She went into the living room with its tattered furnishings, passed into the dining room to round the scarred table, which hadn't seen a happy family dinner in all the years she'd lived there, and then stalled in front of the swinging door to the kitchen.

A rush of something that seemed to be a mixture of stress, fear, anxiousness and almost unbearable excitement overwhelmed her.

She took another deep breath, reminded herself to be cool, that Clint was only an old acquaintance and that getting this over with would make her feel better.

But still it took her a long moment before she worked up the courage to go into the kitchen.

''Oh, good, you're just in time for breakfast,'' Ivey said, when all eyes turned to Savannah as she went through the swinging door she'd been hiding behind.

Ivey, Cully and Clint all sat around the wobbly, square Formica table with steaming cups of coffee and plates laden with cinnamon rolls in front of them.

"Morning," Savannah greeted, glancing more at her sister than at either of the Culhane men, who—along with the third brother, Yance—bore a striking resemblance to each other.

"Mornin'," Cully said cheerfully.

"Savannah," was all Clint said. Too tonelessly for her to get anything from the simple utterance. But he did smile. A small, tentative smile that she caught out of the corner of her eye.

And yet just the sound of her name on his lips, the bare glimpse of that tiny smile, was enough to make her stomach do a jig.

"Come and sit down," Ivey invited.

There was only one chair vacant around the decrepit kitchen table, and it was directly across from Clint. Even though it put them more in line with each other than one of the other chairs might have, Savannah had no choice but to sit there as her sister served her coffee and a roll.

Not that she could eat any of the roll. Her throat was so constricted with tension, she knew she wouldn't be able to swallow food. The best she could hope for was to get some of the coffee down so no one would notice how on edge she was.

"We were just talking about what the guys are doing today," Ivey said to fill her in.

Cully seemed to go on with something he'd been saying before, outlining what he and Clint had planned.

Savannah didn't absorb much of it. She was too aware of Clint. Of his watching her.

He wasn't exactly staring at her. But he wasn't paying attention to what his brother was saying, either. Instead his glance kept traveling from his cup to Savannah; from his half-eaten cinnamon roll to Savannah; from Ivey or Cully to Savannah.

She knew this not only because she kept catching him at it, but also because it was as if his gaze emitted heat. Heat that raised her own temperature a degree or two. That made her feel flushed. That left her oddly aware of the surface of her own skin.

Second cups of coffee were served, more rolls were eaten, and all without either Savannah or Clint saying anything to each other. Savannah began to think that maybe they still weren't going to actually speak. That maybe this encounter was going to be like those through the funeral, where being in the same vicinity still hadn't caused any interaction.

Didn't Clint *want* to talk to her? she began to wonder. Was he as uncomfortable with their being together again as she was? Or was this a big deal only to her? Maybe it was nothing to him. Maybe *she* was so much of nothing to him that he didn't feel the need to bother.

And then all of a sudden Cully stood up.

"Well, come on. We'd better get out there," he said to his brother, catching Savannah off guard because she hadn't been paying attention to anything but the turmoil going on inside her and the man who was causing it. It had left her unaware that what was going on around her had come to a conclusion.

"Right," Clint agreed. "Go ahead and do the

goodbyes I know you and Ivey are gonna do, and I'll be right with you.''

Ivey and Cully laughed, and Ivey stood, too, to walk her fiancé out to the mudroom.

And suddenly Savannah was alone in the kitchen with Clint.

It had seemed to be by design on his part since he could have just gone out ahead of the engaged couple. Which made Savannah expect him to say something.

But he didn't. Not right away. He just stared openly at her, as if Ivey and Cully's being gone gave him the freedom to relearn the way she looked.

It didn't help Savannah's stress level.

But two could play that game, she decided, raising her gaze to finally look straight at him.

And once she'd gone that far she was sunk.

Nothing on earth could have torn her eyes from him as she studied his face the way she'd been studying his body from the upstairs window.

Good Lord, but the years had been kind to him. He'd been great looking as a teenager but the maturity of being thirty-six had taken the Culhane features that Clint, Cully and Yance all shared and chiseled Clint's into a leaner, sharper, more rustic version of his younger self. A strikingly handsome, leaner, sharper, more rustic version.

His nose was somewhat on the long, thin side and took a small rise through the bridge, but that single imperfection only added an earthy touch to what might otherwise have been too flawless.

The sun had left a few lines here and there—across his forehead, at the corners of his eyes—but the lines added to his appeal, contributing character and a pure, rugged masculinity.

He had high cheekbones. Well-defined brows. Skin that was weather-kissed smooth. And eyes. Oh, those eyes...

The Culhane brothers had the same color eyes. They were known for them. Crystal blue. Pale. Clear. Almost colorless.

But none were as beautiful to Savannah as Clint's were.

She'd never forgotten those eyes. But somehow over the years they'd dimmed in her memory. Now she saw again how absolutely gorgeous they were, losing herself for a moment in their depths.

Until she let her gaze slide down to his lips as her mind, for some reason, wandered in that same direction.

Straight, subtle, sensual lips. The lower one fuller than the upper. Soft, warm, adept...

Were they still as masterful? As skillful? As terrific at kissing? she wondered, as her gaze stuck there.

Or were they even better?

"So," she said because she had to pull herself out of her admiring reverie some way. "How have you been?"

He didn't answer immediately. He went on studying her, apparently in no hurry to speak.

Then he said, "I've been okay. Yourself?"

"Good. I've been good." But she would feel better now, if he didn't seem so formal. So removed. So much as if she really was only an old acquaintance he hadn't given any thought to in years and years.

"You look good," he said.

"Thanks. So do you."

"I like your hair long."

"Me, too."

And that seemed to exhaust their subject matter.

Silence fell again.

Clint finally averted his gaze to his coffee cup, turning it round and round in his massive hand with its broad back and long, thick fingers.

Savannah wished he would stop. Not that the action was particularly annoying. It was just that it made her remember the touch of that same hand on her skin. The gentleness. The power held in check even then. The arousal it could induce...

This time it was Clint who saved her from her thoughts.

He nodded in the direction of the mudroom where Ivey and Cully were kissing goodbye and said, "Funny thing to have those two gettin' together like this, isn't it?"

"Pretty strange," she agreed.

"Cully's really in love with her, though. So are the kids. All Amy and Randa can talk about is Ivey. They want to be just like her."

"How old did Ivey tell me Cully's little girls are?"

"Amy's four and Randa is three."

"Ah, that's right. Well, Ivey loves them, too. She'll be a good mother to them."

Good, good, good. Everything was good.

Except the way Savannah felt.

Why wasn't she thrilled that they were making conversation? That they were crossing the bridge to being friendly again, even if it was just with small talk? Why was she suffering some kind of absurd disappointment that it was like this, rather than anything remotely like that fantasy she'd had upstairs?

"You comin'?" Cully called from the mudroom just then, the lovers' goodbyes apparently over.

"Sure," Clint answered. But he didn't move. He stayed where he was a little longer, continuing to look at Savannah.

She wondered if he was trying to realign this new version of her face with his memories of the old.

Or maybe he was trying to figure something out—because that's what his expression seemed to convey. Although that perception could have been only her conscience talking. And the fear that if he looked close enough he might be able to see into her soul. To see the secret she'd kept from him.

"Well, let's get to it, then," Cully urged when Clint didn't hop to.

Clint finally stood, unfolding all six feet three inches of lean, hard-muscled body to tower above Savannah where she sat. And still he kept those glorious eyes trained on her.

"It's kind of nice to have you back in town," he said then.

Only *kind of* nice? she thought.

But of course she didn't say that. Instead she lied and said, "It's nice to be back. For a little while, anyway."

And why had she felt the need to add that footnote? Especially in the tone that had come out sounding like some sort of warning.

"Guess a little while is better than nothin'," he said, giving her a nod and heading out of the kitchen.

Her gaze went with him...hooked to the back pockets of his jeans and feeding her brain a picture of one of the best male rumps she'd ever seen, even as she tried not to notice it. Or appreciate it.

"Be seein' you around," he said over his shoulder.

Savannah shot her eyes upward, uncertain whether or not he'd realized what she was looking at.

"Sure. See you around," she said in a rush, feeling like an idiot.

He paused in the doorway, pivoted on the heels of his cowboy boots and faced her once more, looking at her as if he needed that second glance to convince himself she was real.

He smiled again then. More genuinely than before and big enough to show her the dimples that grinning put dead center in both his cheeks.

How she'd loved those dimples!

And suddenly a memory flashed through her mind of what it had felt like to dip her finger into the indentation of one of them and follow the crease that led to his jaw. His beard hadn't been too coarse before, or really more than a shadow. But now—even though he was clean shaven—she could tell it would feel different. Now it was a man's beard, not a boy's.

Those thoughts were enough to set her pulse racing once more. To make something inside her light up. Something that should have stayed dark.

And then he was gone, out the back door, his deep voice and Cully's fading in the distance as they hashed out the order of the day's work.

"I can't go through with this," Savannah muttered to herself.

"You can't go through with what?" Ivey asked,

clearly having heard her as she returned to the kitchen.

"I don't know how I'm going to stay in Elk Creek and meet up with Clint over and over again."

"It didn't seem so bad."

"Maybe not on the outside."

"I know what's going through your head. But it all happened fifteen years ago. That's forever. And the only thing Clint knew was that we did what we'd always planned to do—we left home as soon as we could get out together. He can't have any idea about the rest, so there's no reason for you to feel awkward and self-conscious."

And sad. She'd have felt sad if what Ivey was talking about had been what was on her mind, because thinking about the events of so long ago always made her feel sad.

But for once her sister was reading her wrong.

It hadn't been the past that had been torturing her this time.

It had been the present.

Seeing Clint. Appreciating what she saw. Feeling as attracted to him as she had so many years back.

But she didn't let Ivey know the real route her thoughts had taken. Instead she just said, "This is not going to be easy."

Ivey smiled as if she knew something Savannah didn't. "But maybe it'll be worth it."

## Chapter Two

"You've been awful quiet today."

Ranch work didn't stop even on Sundays, so Clint and Yance—the eldest Culhane brother at thirty-seven—had been tending to the animals in their own barn all morning, when Yance made that observation of Clint.

Clint was in one of the stalls, brushing down Lucille, more often referred to as the red mare. Yance had apparently finished up for the day because he was leaning idly on the end pole—something he wouldn't have done until his chores were taken care of.

"Somethin' botherin' you?" he asked Clint.

"Nah," Clint lied.

His brother persisted, anyway. "Cully says you had a few minutes alone with Savannah Heller yesterday."

"A few. But not really what you'd call alone. Cully and Ivey were just sayin' their goodbyes a couple of feet away."

"So how'd it go?"

"Cully and Ivey sayin' goodbye?" Clint asked, being purposely obtuse because he wasn't anxious to discuss Savannah or anything to do with her.

"No. You know I was talkin' about how those few minutes alone with Savannah Heller went," Yance clarified tenaciously.

"No big deal. We exchanged some small talk. That's it."

"You've been waitin' for her a long time. She's finally back, you were alone with her, and all you did was exchange small talk?"

"I haven't been *waitin'* for her," Clint said testily.

"Seemed that way."

"Well, it wasn't. And what was I supposed to do? Throw her across the kitchen table and hop on?"

"Bet that's what you wanted to do."

"What I wanted to do was ask a few questions."

"So why didn't you?"

"It just didn't work out that way."

Clint hadn't so much as paused in his grooming of the red mare to look at his brother, but from the corner of his eye he saw Yance nod.

"Maybe it'll work out better tonight at the engagement dinner," the older Culhane suggested with an edge of goading in his tone.

"Yeah. Maybe," Clint answered as if he didn't much care.

Yance pushed off the post and headed out of the barn. But he didn't seem able to resist throwing one last comment over his shoulder as he went. "And then maybe the *waitin'* will finally be over for you."

Clint chuckled drolly at his brother's teasing but he didn't respond. He just went on brushing the horse. But he started thinking about Savannah again the moment Yance had left.

Of course, thinking about Savannah was nothing new. Not since he'd spotted her at Bucky Dennehy's funeral. Clint had been thinking about her almost nonstop since then.

Hell, who was he kidding? Savannah had been on his mind almost nonstop since he'd heard Ivey had come back to town two weeks ago.

And in the fifteen years before that?

Savannah hadn't been on his mind nonstop, but the truth of it was that she'd spent a fair share of time there.

Not that that meant he'd been waiting for her the way Yance had said. He hadn't been. Only a fool would have done something like that. But there was no denying she had her own spot in his head. Maybe in his heart, too.

That wasn't so unusual, he assured himself. Savannah had been his first love. Everybody held their first love as special. That's all there was to it.

And, man, had he loved that girl!

Sure, they'd been barely more than kids who'd gotten together at the end of their senior year of high school. Some would say that meant any feelings they'd had for each other were only puppy love. But those people would be mistaken. Because what he'd felt for Savannah had been a lot more than that.

It had been enough to keep them together through

the two years after graduation until Ivey had finished school, too, and she and Savannah had left Elk Creek. And it had been enough to keep the memory of Savannah lingering around the edges of his mind since then.

No, not just puppy love. His feelings for her had been strong. Stronger, apparently, than her feelings for him had been, because hers hadn't been strong enough to keep her here.

But that had all been a long time ago. So long ago it was ancient history.

At least it *should* have been ancient history.

But now that she was back, his old feelings for her were hinting at having some life left in them. Ancient history or not.

Damn, but he hated that fact! Hated that it put so much as a drop of credence in Yance's belief that, on some level, Clint had been waiting for Savannah all along. Hated that a woman who'd taken off the way she had could still stir something up in him.

But there it was.

It had only taken seeing her again across a roomful of mourners to let him know he was as attracted to her as he'd been as a randy kid.

She looked even better than she had fifteen years ago.

Long hair suited her. It feminized her. It gave her a softness that the chopped-off, sheep-shears cut her father had insisted on hadn't.

And had her hair always been such a reddish blond color? Either Clint had forgotten or he hadn't noticed it much because it had been so short.

But now her hair had been the first thing to catch

his eye at the funeral. Long, straight, silky hair. Hanging free, shining luminously. He'd wanted to run his fingers through it. He'd wanted to know if it was as soft and luxurious to the touch as it looked.

And then there were her eyes. Oh, yeah, the eyes were grabbers, too.

They were lighter than her sister's. More the shade of the flowers that grew on the lilac bush beside the Culhanes' house. Lavender with a hint of blue to them. And lashes that were so long, so thick, they actually cast shadows over the clear, bright, dewy depths of those eyes.

Naturally beautiful, that's what Savannah was. It was what she'd always been, though all that time ago her beauty had been less striking.

He'd taken a lot of ribbing for dating one of Silas Heller's "sons" as Ivey and Savannah had been known behind their backs. Their father hadn't allowed them anything in the way of clothes or hairstyles that would have pegged them as the girls they were. He'd forced them to be such tomboys that some folks mistook them both for male.

But the attraction between Clint and Savannah had had as much to do with pure chemistry as with any appearance. Chemistry so potent that when he'd taken notice of her, working beside her, painting the house of an elderly woman who belonged to their same church, he'd bucked popular opinion and asked Savannah out. He'd gotten to know her, at the time, more for the person she was than for how she'd looked.

But that didn't mean he didn't appreciate the way she looked now.

Much as he wished he were impervious to it.

She had skin like alabaster with rose-petal cheeks and only a sprinkling of freckles across a nose she tilted into the air when her spirit was showing. And lips that went along for the ride—slightly full, pink lips that reflected a strong will.

Lips he'd wanted to kiss so badly in the kitchen the previous day that he'd had to take a firm hand in reminding himself that things were not the way they used to be, that he and Savannah hardly knew each other anymore, that he shouldn't even be *thinking* about kissing her, that he had to keep himself and his thoughts under control.

But it had been a tough task.

Especially since she'd filled out some, too—in all the right places. She was still willowy, to be sure, but now there were more curves where they were supposed to be. Luscious, soft curves.

Nope, nobody would be mistaking her for a boy these days....

The red mare whinnied and turned its head to nudge Clint's shin, right then. His attention had wandered so completely to Savannah that he must have paused in mid-stroke.

He went back to work, saying, "Sorry, Lucille," and was glad neither of his brothers had been there to see his lapse.

Sure as shootin', they'd have known what he was thinking. And given him a hard time about it.

But not only would they have razzed him. He knew they'd have urged him to pursue some things with Savannah, too. To explore what had been so abruptly and prematurely ended fifteen years ago. To see if it was possible to rekindle it now.

Not that he was interested in rekindling anything.

"But there *is* some unfinished business," he admitted to the mare.

As he'd told Yance, he had some questions for Miss Savannah Heller. Questions he'd carried around for too damn long now.

Like why had she suddenly—and for no reason he'd ever understood—kept her distance from him the final two weeks before leaving Elk Creek with Ivey.

Like what had happened to all their talk about marriage and her staying here so they could build a life together.

And most of all, what he wanted to know was why, when she did leave, it had been without so much as telling him goodbye....

Yeah, they had more to say to each other than small talk, all right.

He just wished it wasn't so hard for him to remember it. One look at her and the past seemed to withdraw into the distance while his senses feasted on Savannah herself.

And when that happened, he could think only about what it would take for him to be able to reach out and touch her. Pull her into his arms. Breathe in the sweet scent of her that he could still smell whenever he closed his eyes and let it waft through his memory....

The horse whinnied a second time, and only then did Clint realize he *had* closed his eyes. That he was standing there lost in his own meandering thoughts yet again.

He sighed in disgust with himself and went back to grooming the horse.

But somehow, as he drew the brush along the rise of the animal's hind quarter, he started imagining smoothing his hand over the small mound of Savannah's rear end. Longingly. Lovingly...

"Damn," he muttered to himself.

Being attracted to her wasn't going to make anything easier. It certainly wouldn't help him resolve the history between them that cried out for resolving.

But he had to try. Now that he had the chance, he had to ask his questions. He had to hear the answers.

And after that?

He didn't know.

He guessed he'd just go from there.

And hope for the best.

Although he didn't know what the best was.

He knew only that the old attraction was alive and well and living deep down inside him, whether he liked it or not.

And that it was nagging at him to do something about it.

Savannah had come to Elk Creek for a funeral, not for a wedding, so the clothes she'd brought with her were few and far from festive. To get herself through the celebrations and the extended stay, she'd had to buy a few things from Elk Creek's sole women's clothing store.

But as she surveyed them late Sunday afternoon, trying to figure out what to wear to Ivey and Cully's engagement dinner, she wasn't bowled over by any of her purchases.

She reminded herself that the dinner wouldn't be terribly fancy. Her cousins—Jackson, Linc and Beth—were giving it at the ranch house Jackson lived in across the road. Only the Heller family and the Culhanes had been invited, since it seemed inappropriate to have a big party so soon after the death of a close friend to them all. But in spite of the size of the celebration, and the fact that it was mainly family, and that her options were limited, Savannah still couldn't decide what to wear.

Maybe it was because she was dreading the evening, she thought, as she stood beside her bed where all the possible outfits were laid out.

Or maybe it was because along with that dread, there was also a bubbling cauldron of excitement in her.

How the two could exist together was something she didn't understand. But then there were a lot of things she didn't understand these days. She herself was at the top of the list.

Fretting over every detail. Over what she would talk about. Over how to act. None of that was common for her. Savannah was a take-me-or-leave-me-as-I-am kind of person.

Or at least she had been until now.

But now she was as giddy as a kid at Christmas, over just the prospect of seeing Clint. Giddy and worried and eager and excited and even all atingle.

And she didn't want to be any of those things. She *shouldn't* be any of those things.

Why couldn't she head for this dinner without giving Clint a second thought? she asked herself. Why couldn't she wear any old thing without considering whether or not he might like it?

No matter how hard she tried, though, she couldn't look at the clothes and not wonder what might impress him the most. What might make his eyes pop right out of his head. What might make his jaw drop and send him home with visions of her that would haunt him through the night.

And the truth was that none of what she'd brought with her or been able to buy in the small-town store was likely to do any of those things.

The things laid out on her bed were pretty, nice, sensible, conservative clothes. Just the sort of things she had at home in Cheyenne. Just the sort of things she always bought and wore. And they had looked good on her when she'd tried them on in the dressing room.

But nothing among them was going to turn her into more than she was.

And for the first time in her life, she wished she'd paid more attention to how to be a slinky, sexy knock-out. A woman who could walk into a room and make all heads turn.

A woman who would make Clint Culhane sit up and take notice so entirely that he wouldn't even be aware there was anyone else in the room.

What in the world had gotten into her?

Wasn't it bad enough that she hadn't been able to think about anything but Clint since the minute she'd arrived back in Elk Creek? Wasn't it bad enough that she'd replayed in her mind every word, every nuance, every gesture, every expression, every moment of the scant hello they'd finally exchanged the day before?

Wasn't it enough that she couldn't get his image out of her mind? That every time she sat down to work, that every time she tried to sleep, her mind's eye flashed up a picture of Clint? Of those gorgeous crystal blue eyes? Of that chiseled face? Of that big, muscular body? Of those masculine hands and sensual lips and those to-die-for dimples?

Did she have to be so attracted to him that she lost sight of herself? That she wanted to turn herself into something she wasn't?

Apparently she *did* have to, because no matter how hard she tried, she couldn't stop herself.

Any more than she could stop the butterflies in her stomach when she counted down how long it would be before she got to see Clint again.

Any more than she could stop the fantasies that kept playing themselves out in her mind of what she would say to him, of what he might say to her, of how they might find a moment alone and how it might be so much better than the day before because now the ice had been broken—

"You're not dressed yet?"

Ivey's voice interrupted Savannah's musings.

Savannah hadn't heard her sister come into the bedroom, and the sudden sound startled her.

When she'd caught her breath, she said, "I can't decide what to wear."

"You? You always just throw something on and go."

"I know."

"But now you're going to see Clint, and just anything won't do," Ivey guessed.

"No, that's not it."

"Like fun it isn't," Ivey said, as if she were delighted to see Savannah's turmoil over this.

Which spurred Savannah to prove her sister was wrong. She snatched up a form-fitting, mid-calf-length dress with a flared skirt and slipped it on.

"I'm just not in love with any of these things we found in town," she declared as she buttoned the two dozen buttons that went from the V neckline of its black velvet collar to the hem of the royal blue wool dress.

"That dress is great and so are the other things you bought. They aren't the problem," Ivey persisted. "The problem is that you're afraid to be around Clint Culhane."

"I'm not afraid of anything."

"Are, too," Ivey joked, making this conversation sound like it might have when they were kids. "Are, too. Are, too," she repeated in a singsong as she picked up the shoes she'd obviously come into the room to get in the first place and left again.

"Am not," Savannah called after her with a laugh.

But the truth was that Ivey was partially right.

Not that Savannah was afraid of Clint.

What she was afraid of was all the feelings that were awakening inside her like tiny tulips sprouting in early spring from bulbs planted long before that.

Feelings she didn't want to bud, along with an attraction she didn't want to have to a man she'd left behind. A man she'd left behind in a way she considered dishonorable.

But there they were—the feelings and the attraction.

And she didn't know what to do with them.

"Ignore them," she muttered as if she were giving advice to someone else.

Good advice, though, she thought.

Just because a person had feelings or an attraction to someone didn't mean that that person had to act on them.

She might not be able to control what was going on inside her, but she could control what she did about it.

And what she was going to do about it was nothing.

Absolutely nothing at all.

Except make sure the feelings and the attraction were hidden from Clint.

And everyone else, too.

And then maybe the feelings and the attraction would go away.

At least she hoped they would.

It just didn't help that Clint was so incredibly...Clint. Handsome. Masculine. Slightly wry. Laid-back. In command. Sexy.

Savannah's thoughts drifted into another of those fantasies until she caught herself at it again and fought it off.

No matter how difficult it was, she vowed to herself, she was going to keep a level head. She would get through Ivey's wedding as best she could, being polite and civil to Clint, not spending any more time with him than necessary and holding a tight rein on her emotions.

And then she'd go home. Gladly. To Cheyenne. To the small but comfortable apartment she and Ivey had shared until so recently. To the work she loved. To her orderly everyday life.

She just had to hope that those thoughts and feelings didn't go home with her.

Savannah and Ivey's father, Silas Heller, had a brother, Shag, the father of Jackson, Linc and Beth. Shag had been the more successful of the two ranchers, so while Savannah and Ivey's family home was small, the place in which their cousins had been raised was much grander.

In spite of being built in the style of a mountain cabin with split logs and mortar, it was still a two-story, H-shaped, sprawling home set away from the road on a long, paved drive that formed a circle in front.

For the occasion of the engagement dinner, the cousins had decorated the place inside and out. Outside, tiny white Christmas lights had been strung from the eaves and lined the cobbled courtyard that nestled within the arms of the H.

Inside, there was more candlelight than electrical light, and fresh wildflowers were set in vases throughout the foyer, the sunken living room and the enormous dining room.

Once Savannah had finally managed to dress and find just the right earrings—very thin, small gold hoops—she'd gone over to the house to help however she could. Her cousins were already there, so she joined Jackson, his wife, Ally, and stepdaughter, Meggie; Beth and her husband, Ash Blackwolf, and their infant daughter, Melissa; and Linc, his young son, Danny, and his wife, Kansas, who was also sister to the recently widowed Della Dennehy. Della was

Savannah's oldest friend and the reason she'd come back to Elk Creek in the first place.

"Della decided not to come?" Savannah asked Kansas as they headed out of the kitchen carrying appetizers set to go on the coffee table in the living room.

"She appreciated the invitation but—"

"She was afraid she'd be a drag on the party," Savannah guessed.

"She wasn't really up to it, either. Plus she had a lot to do getting all four kids ready to leave for Phoenix with our folks at dawn tomorrow."

"You and Ivey and I are still going over in the afternoon to help her sort through Bucky's things and get her ready to go to Phoenix herself, aren't we?"

"She's counting on it," Kansas said as she put a tray of canapés down and tried to make room for what Savannah was still holding.

The doorbell rang just then, and that was all it took for Savannah's heart to skip a beat, and her eyes to shoot to the front door.

The cousins wouldn't hear of Ivey doing any of the work for the dinner and had insisted she stay across the road until Cully picked her up so they could come together. Whether or not that meant the whole Culhane clan would arrive along with them, Savannah didn't know. But it didn't matter. The mere possibility that Clint could be standing just outside was enough for her composure to slip.

Jackson came from upstairs at the sound of the bell and opened the door as both Savannah and Kansas watched. In walked Ivey, Cully and Cully's two preschool-age daughters—Amy and Randa. They were followed by Yance and finally Clint.

It didn't take more than one glance at him for Savannah to get so jittery that the bowl of vegetable dip on the crystal dish she was holding clattered in her hands.

Kansas looked at the dishes and then up to Savannah's face, laughed and teased, "Ah, I see somebody among the Culhanes has the power to disturb you. I wonder which one it could be?"

Savannah didn't respond to that. She just set the vegetable-laden plate and dip bowl on the table and hid her hands in the folds of her skirt.

*Get a grip on yourself,* she silently ordered, trying to look at anyone but Clint.

But her traitorous eyes wouldn't obey.

They barely brushed over everybody else and attached themselves squarely on the middle Culhane brother.

Clint was dressed in a crisp, white Western shirt with a string tie adorning the front of it. Below that, a pair of new-looking snakeskin boots poked out from beneath well-cut charcoal gray jeans that hugged narrow hips and flashed a belt buckle the size of a lemon above the zipper.

The zipper she had no business looking anywhere in the direction of....

Savannah yanked her gaze upward, wishing she could look away from him completely. But failing that, she settled her eyes above his collar.

His hair still had that carefree look, and he was clean shaven. So clean shaven that she had the most awful urge to go to him, to get close enough to tell if he was wearing aftershave and smelled as good as he looked.

To defeat that urge she said a general hello and ducked back into the kitchen.

That set a course of avoidance that she followed throughout the next few hours. When she couldn't hide in the kitchen, she made sure her only contact with Clint was as part of the group, never speaking directly to him, never venturing anywhere near him. But there wasn't a moment that she wasn't more conscious of him than of anyone else at the party...of how terrifically good-looking he was showered and shaved and cleaned up. Of the deep, deep timbre of his voice. The low rumble of his laughter.

She knew that she was drawing more than her fair share of his attention, too, because she could feel his eyes on her through the whole meal they all enjoyed around the enormous dining table. And each time she glanced in his direction she found him studying her, not even trying to hide it.

Being overly conscious of him was one thing. But being under his scrutiny was something else. It made her terribly uneasy, and as warm as if his eyes actually could produce heat. By the time the meal was finished, the table cleared and the kids dispatched to another room to watch a movie, Savannah desperately needed to cool off, and she didn't think an after-dinner drink would do the trick.

Ivey and Cully were the center of attention, so it was easy enough for Savannah to slip into the kitchen and through one of the sliding glass doors out to the back patio, where the brick-paved expanse was bare of the furniture that occupied the space during the summer months. More of the tiny white lights had been strung from the house to the big brick barbecue pit, through the naked branches of the old black oak trees, around the empty pool and full circle to the house again.

In the soft glow of their lights Savannah took a deep breath and held it as long as she could before exhaling. Then, feeling better, she wandered out to the barbecue, enjoying the quiet, the coolness, the freedom from the internal turmoil caused by being near Clint.

When she'd reached the barbecue she turned her back to it, leaned her hips against the edge and raised the heel of her shoe to hook onto the decorative ledge that circled it about eighteen inches from the ground. Then she raised her face to the sky and stared at the stars.

Peaceful. It was so peaceful out there—a feeling she'd never really connected with anything about Elk Creek before.

Growing up there hadn't been a peaceful time for either her or Ivey. Not under the heavy hand of Silas Heller, who hadn't been what anyone would consider a loving father.

But it was peaceful there now, she realized, thinking that maybe her sister was right, that being in the small town again was a much different—much improved—experience than it had been all those years ago, when their father was alive.

*No wonder Ivey's happy about moving back,* Savannah thought.

If it wasn't for Clint being in Elk Creek, she might have considered moving back herself.

If it wasn't for Clint and what had happened just before she'd left the small town originally....

"Are you hidin' out here?"

If the first sight of Clint entering the house had made her jittery, the sound of his voice coming suddenly out of the night startled her so much she nearly went apoplectic. Her insides took a leap, her back straightened, her eyes shot toward the house and adrenaline wiped away her short-lived calm.

"Hiding? No, I'm not hiding," she said in a hurry, her nervousness echoing in her too-innocent tone.

All she could think of was that being alone with him was worse than being in the house, with everyone else acting as a buffer between them. She said, "I just needed a little fresh air. Now I'm ready to go in again."

She pushed away from the barbecue so she could make a run for the safety of the party. But in taking her heel from the ledge, it caught on her hem and stuck.

Precariously balanced, she hopped sideways like a one-legged kangaroo, trying to free herself and not fall into the barbecue pit she was headed for.

Just in the nick of time, Clint rushed the last few feet that separated them and grabbed her by the arms to steady her before she tumbled into the hole in the ground that was large enough for a full side of beef.

"Okay, now I feel dumb," she muttered to herself without thinking that there was no way he could miss hearing it.

He chuckled softly, and when she looked up she found his handsome face more relaxed than she'd seen it the whole time she'd been back in Elk Creek.

"Clumsy, maybe. But not dumb," he teased, grinning down at her, his dimples at full bore.

The grin was infectious, and before Savannah knew it, she was smiling back and answering his goad. "I am not clumsy," she said, as if meeting some challenge he was throwing out at her.

"I suppose this is just what happens when tomboys wear dresses?"

"Apparently," she said more good-naturedly.

She was beginning to be aware of the feel of his hands on her. Even through her long wool sleeves little sparks of electricity were starting to dance through her nerve endings.

Not a good thing, because it was altogether too nice a sensation. In fact it was making her light-headed.

She reached down quickly to release her hem from her heel while Clint went on supporting her. But even after she could put her other foot on the ground again he didn't let her go. Instead he lifted her as effortlessly as if she were a small child and sat her on the brick edge of the barbecue.

"I've gotcha now," he said, smiling, a wicked glint of mischief showing in his eyes even in the dim white glow of the decorative lights.

He was standing right in front of her, not six inches between them. To her left stretched the whole grill, and on her other side was the pit. So there was no way she could get down without his moving.

And he seemed to have no inclination to do that as he shifted his weight onto one insolent hip and casually crossed his arms over his broad, hard chest.

"We really should go in. We'll be missed," she said, not sure how to answer his "gotcha" comment.

"No one's gonna miss you. You've spent the whole night tryin' to be somewhere else, anyway. Me, now, I've been so much fun that I'll be missed plenty," he joked.

"Then you better go back," she said in a way that sounded too much as if she didn't mean it.

"When I have you where I want you? Not a chance."

She threw a glance at the grate next to her. "You want to grill me?" she asked, making it sound like a play on words. Actually she was worried that that was just what he wanted to do—grill her about the past.

He seemed to think about that for a moment, as if he were tempted. Then he shook his head. "Not tonight. Not if I can get a few more minutes like this."

She knew what he meant. Since her one-legged kangaroo impression it was as if a wall between them had started crumbling. They were being easier with—and *on*—each other. Almost like old times.

It was dangerous, and Savannah knew it. That wall had made it easier to resist the attraction she had for him. Easier to resist his charm. His smoldering sexiness.

But it was so nice to experience the wall coming down—to feel the good things that being with him like this again made her feel—that she couldn't force herself to erect the barriers again.

"Do you realize," he said with a glance down at her skirt, "that I've never seen you in a dress before tonight?"

"That's because until I left Elk Creek I never owned one. My father wouldn't hear of it."

"Your father..." he said through clenched teeth that conveyed a long-held contempt for the man.

But then Clint seemed to let go of the sentiment and gave Savannah the once-over as if to confirm what he'd been thinking all evening. "Well, you do a dress justice."

"Thank you," she said, much more delighted than she wanted to be at the compliment.

"So. This is twice now we've talked about looks. And yesterday we said how weird it is that Cully and Ivey got together. Shall we discuss the weather now?"

It was nice that the awkwardness that had been between them was dissipating enough for him to make light of it. Savannah played along, looking up at the sky again.

"No clouds. Maybe fifty degrees. Weather's pretty good. What do you want to talk about now?"

"How about you?" he suggested.

"Not much to say about me."

"You could tell me what's been goin' on with you. About bein' a teacher."

"I teach eighth-grade English composition," she said as if that summed up her life.

He groaned the way her students did when she assigned essays.

"It's not *that* bad," she said with a laugh, wanting to put her finger in the dimple that creased only one cheek when he smiled the way he had just then, with only one side of his mouth. And maybe after she'd put her finger in that dimple she'd press her lips to it. Then take a dip with her tongue...

She reined in that unruly thought and added, "I try to make my class interesting."

"Umm-hmm," he moaned as if that weren't possible. "But Ivey tells me you aren't workin' now."

"I'm on leave to write my master's thesis."

He whistled as if he were impressed, then went back to teasing her. "A schoolmarm with a whole slew of degrees—I'd never have guessed that was how you'd end up."

"You make me sound like some kind of old spinster teacher with a pencil poked through my bun."

He made a show of looking at the buns she was sitting on, knowing full well she'd been referring to a hairstyle.

"Nope, no pencils."

"Smart aleck."

"Want to send me to the principal's office?"

She didn't want to send him anywhere. Not when she was enjoying this so much. Enjoying him so much. "I'll just let you off with a warning this time."

"Gee, thanks," he joked, with that dimpled half grin again.

The man was just too gorgeous for her own good, and Savannah wished she could overlook it. But she couldn't. Instead she was getting more and more drawn in.

"I'll bet you run a tight ship," he said then, drawing her out of her reverie yet again.

"A tight ship? Pretty much, yeah, I guess."

"But you probably have so many pubescent boys in love with you that they don't care."

"I've had one or two boys with crushes, but on the

whole I think they're pretty clear about the fact that I don't take any guff.''

"I'd like to give you a little guff," he said under his breath. Then with another of those wicked smiles, he said, "So what do you do on your time off?"

"Oh, a lot of extra things with the kids—chaperoning dances, fund-raising, overseeing the drama club, directing the annual spring play, tutoring—"

Clint groaned even louder. "Man, you *are* a schoolmarm. When do you go out and kick up your heels?"

Rarely. Almost never. But Savannah didn't want to admit that. "I like what I do."

"But all work and no play—"

"Maybe it all feels like play to me."

"Then you're kiddin' yourself," he said with a laugh.

Maybe she was. Because being there like that with him—flirting with him, joking, teasing—was unlike anything she'd done with anyone in longer than she could remember. And it was making her feel better than she had in even longer than that.

"Sounds to me," he added, "like instead of leavin' that nasty-old-man of a father of yours behind when you left Elk Creek, you took him along somewhere inside you to keep you toeing the line and doin' nothin' but work, work, work."

She'd never thought of it like that, but in a way Clint wasn't far off the mark. Her father had been adamantly against any kind of recreation. Wasting time—that's what he had called anything that smacked of amusement.

If Savannah or Ivey weren't at school they were to

be doing ranch chores. If they weren't doing chores, they were to be doing homework. If they weren't doing homework they were to be cleaning the house or preparing his meals. Six hours of sleep a night was the only idle time they had, and he'd have cut that shorter, too, if he could have.

Savannah had had to sneak away to be with Clint. She'd had to pretend she was studying at the library or doing something at school, or meet him out in the fields when her father sent her to mend fences or dig post holes or herd cows.

And how different was her life now? she asked herself suddenly. She taught classes. She ran extracurricular activities. She used her evenings to grade papers or make up lesson plans or prepare for the next day's lecture. Then she went to bed so she could start it all over again the next morning.

Work, work, work.

And no play....

"You know, you might be right," she conceded to Clint with a laugh. "I never realized it, but I am sort of a workaholic."

He shook his head in what looked like mock sadness. "Shame. Maybe while you're here you can cut loose a little."

With him? That was much, much too appealing a thought.

It scared the daylights out of her.

"Oh, I don't think so. There are all the wedding preparations to do, and I can't get behind on my thesis, and there's Della and—"

Clint stopped the flood of excuses with one long

index finger pressed to her mouth. "Maybe I need to teach the teacher to relax."

She reared back and closed her hand around his thick wrist to pull his finger away. "I don't think that would be a good idea," she said in what sounded almost like panic. Probably because panic was what she felt to think of Clint taking her under his wing in anything. Panic at how much she might like it. And where it might lead.

Undaunted by the hand that held him at bay, he replaced his finger at her lips with his nose nearly tip to tip with hers, his blue eyes boring into her. "You afraid of me these days, Savannah?" he asked, as if he found that idea very amusing.

"Of course not," she said. Weakly. The clean, woodsy scent of his aftershave wafted around her. Her temperature was rising remarkably yet again. Her skin was tingling. Her insides were all atwitter.

And memories of what it had been like to be kissed by him were flashing through her mind as if it had been yesterday....

"I just don't have time for fooling around," she added, wishing belatedly that she'd used a less innuendo-laden phrase.

Clint caught it and bestowed that wicked grin once more. "Maybe we'll have to make time."

"Seems like making time with me is what you're already trying to do," she countered, a bit of her old spunk creeping back in at the last minute to save her.

Clint straightened away from her to laugh, a barrel-deep boom that echoed with pure masculinity. "I never could put one over on you, could I?"

Did that mean he'd only been teasing her?

Savannah didn't know and couldn't ask. Not without seeming as if she was disappointed that he might have been just joking.

But she *was* disappointed.

She hated that fact. Hated how high her hopes had leaped at the thought that maybe Clint Culhane was, after all, bent on doing a little courting. A little wooing. Maybe a little rekindling—

"We probably should go in," she said then, nodding toward the house where she thought she'd be safe from the wild thoughts and feelings going on inside her.

Clint glanced over one mile-wide shoulder in the same direction, then looked at her again. "I guess so," he agreed. And why did that compound her disappointment to no end?

He finally stepped back, holding out a hand to help her down.

She knew she wouldn't be able to accept that hand and not feel more of those electrical sparks from his touch, but she didn't know how to refuse without making a big deal out of it.

So she slipped her hand in his and suffered—well, not quite *suffered*—that sensation again.

But as soon as she was down she pulled her hand away.

"So do you think you could stop being so hell-bent on steering clear of me?" he asked. "I'm beginnin' to feel like a leper."

"I just thought it might be best for us to keep our distance."

"Probably is. But I'd still like it if you wouldn't do it."

He admitted that in a quiet voice that Savannah thought spoke of some of the same internal tug-of-war she was having over what she knew she should do and what her attraction to him was nudging her toward.

"I can't make any promises," she told him.

"And I can't make any promises not to follow you, even if you do keep dodging me, which will make it a waste of your energy."

She took that warning without saying anything because by then they were back in the house, back with everyone else, and drawn apart again. But still those blue eyes of his stayed on her, as if letting her know he really couldn't stand for her to put too much distance between them.

Which would not help matters any.

Because throughout the remainder of the evening and on into the night as Savannah lay wide-awake in her bed, she kept thinking about that moment when Clint's nose had been pressed to hers. When his mouth had been only a breath away. When she'd been remembering vividly what it had been like to be kissed by him long ago.

Only in it all there was something besides memories tormenting her. She was lost in a burning curiosity about what it might be like to have Clint Culhane kiss her now.

So if he kept on closing the distance she tried to put between them, she was probably in trouble. For no matter how hard she tried, she couldn't help wishing for some satisfaction to that burning curiosity.

And his being nearby made the possibility of it happening, the possibility of her giving in to it, all the more real.

## Chapter Three

Clint was staring at the ceiling of his bedroom long before his alarm was set to go off the next morning. He was lying on his back, his hands clasped behind his head, and there was only one thing on his mind to disturb his sleep: Savannah.

He'd followed her outside the night before to ask some of the questions that were still troubling him. But catching her when she'd almost fallen, touching her, having her finally smile at him, had put the questions on hold.

It had been too good to see her like that, to joke with her, to have some of the tension that had been between them dissolve. He hadn't been able to make himself ruin it all by probing into the past. So he hadn't.

Instead he'd acted as if they'd just met at a class reunion. And he'd let himself enjoy her company.

But the questions still needed to be asked.

Even more of them than he'd had before.

Because her being in Elk Creek again seemed to renew all the things he'd wondered about, worried about, asked himself when she'd left. Things that, over the years, he'd managed to bury.

They were all cropping up now like stickweeds in a wheat field. Had he somehow hurt her? Had he driven her away without knowing how or why? Had he taken her for granted after two years of dating and caused her feelings for him to change? What the hell had he done wrong?

Something. There had to have been something.

And maybe if he could find out what it was, he could fix it....

Yeah, that was where those thoughts kept leading him, like it or not. And he wasn't sure he did like it.

*Should* he try to fix whatever it was that had gone bad between him and Savannah? What was the point of that unless he was wanting to start things up with her again?

And how smart would *that* be?

Sure, he was still so attracted to her that, even now, he knew it wouldn't take much to get involved with her. In the blink of an eye. Head-over-heels involved.

But he would be head-over-heels involved with a woman who had left him without a word. Who hadn't cared for him enough to even let him know the reasons she'd switched from talking marriage one day to not answering his calls, not seeing him, the next.

Why would anyone be so much of a glutton for

punishment that they would sign on for a second round that could well end the same way? It would be like voluntarily sticking his neck in a noose.

On the other hand, he didn't know if he could actually stop himself.

Yes, the drive to know what had happened was strong. Maybe the ego Savannah had bruised was playing a part in that, an ego that wanted to know why he hadn't been able to keep the woman he loved.

But the urge to find out what had gone wrong so he could repair it was even stronger. Because he was just plain drawn to her. Every bit as much as he had been before. So drawn to her that the previous evening, when he'd had the perfect opportunity to get some answers to his questions, he hadn't. Instead he'd opted for just reveling in being alone with her.

Nothing else had seemed more important than that at the time. Just the way nothing but being with her had seemed important fifteen years ago.

Whatever it was that drew him to her was powerful. As powerful now as it had been when he'd been a randy, rowdy, hell-raising teenager who'd calmed down the minute Savannah had caught his eye.

There had been something so soft beneath her tomboy exterior. A vulnerability that had struck him as a challenge to bring it out in her.

And beautiful? The closer he'd gotten to her the more he'd realized just how beautiful she really was. So naturally beautiful that he'd wondered how he'd ever missed it before. The kind of luminous beauty that didn't need makeup or fancy hairstyles.

And when she'd smiled? It was as if the sun had risen right there around her....

None of that had dimmed over all these years. That was part of the problem in fighting off his attraction to her. In fact, she was more appealing now, without the oppression of an ornery old cuss of a father holding her back.

And Clint was anything but immune to that appeal. It knocked the wind out of him. Knocked the questions out of his mind, even as it left him ready to put his neck in that noose to find out what had gone wrong fifteen years ago, to make amends for it and maybe see if there could be anything between them again.

His alarm clock went off just then and he reached over to stop it, checked the time and realized he'd been lying there thinking about Savannah for more than an hour.

But he still didn't have any answers. Not to the questions he needed to pose to her. Not to the questions he kept asking himself.

Maybe he was just a damn fool.

A fool for Savannah Heller. Who had dumped him, deserted him. And not even let him know why.

Only a fool would go after a woman who had done that to him once already. But foolish or not, he knew deep down that he was going to ask his questions of her. That he was going to try to right whatever had gone wrong. That he was going to pursue her.

Because he couldn't help himself. He couldn't stop thinking about her. Picturing her in his mind's eye. Wanting her.

And wanting what they'd had before, too. What had been so terrific, so right, that it should have lasted a lifetime.

And if the questions he asked her had answers he didn't like? Then he'd take his neck out of the noose before it was too late.

But he didn't think any answer she could offer him would make him not want to give this a second chance.

If she'd let him.

And he had to hope she would. He had to hope that finding out what had gone wrong between them would clear the air and make way for exploring the feelings he had for her that had never quite gone away—for exploring the attraction that was as strong, as powerful, as it had been so long ago.

And if he got hurt again?

It was a risk he was willing to take. A risk he was going to take. A risk he didn't have any choice but to take. Because Savannah Heller was under his skin. She'd never stopped being under his skin.

And he just couldn't ignore that.

Not anymore.

Not when she was right next door....


"I feel like somebody has beaten me up," Della Dennehy said with a mirthless laugh as she settled against the front of her sofa and took a sip of wine.

After three hours of sorting through her late husband's clothes and belongings that afternoon, Savannah, Ivey, Kansas and Della had taken a dinner break before finishing up and helping Della pack her things. She was going to join her children and parents in Phoenix for an extended stay to get away from the memories that were rife in her house. Savannah, Ivey and Kansas had volunteered as help and moral support.

The pizza had been delivered—a brand-new convenience to Elk Creek—and when it had arrived they'd opened a bottle of wine and all four had sat on the floor around Della's coffee table to eat.

"I know it's tough," Kansas said to her sister. "But it's good we're getting this done now, so when you and the kids are ready to come home again it can be to a new beginning, without having to face Bucky's things."

Della nodded her agreement but her eyes filled with tears, anyway. She blinked them back and tasted the wine once more before changing the subject—something that had become a pattern throughout the afternoon to get her mind off the sad chore of disposing of what her late husband had left behind.

"So. Savannah," Della said, "how is it, being in Elk Creek again?"

Savannah shrugged as she swallowed a bite of pizza and then said, "In some ways, not as bad as I thought it would be. It's nicer here than I remembered. But I think that just has to do with the fact that dear old dad isn't around to make things ugly."

"If it's not as bad as you thought it would be in some ways, does that mean in other ways it *is* bad to be back?" Kansas asked.

Della laughed for real this time and answered before Savannah could. "It's worse than you thought it would be to see Clint Culhane again, right?"

"Here, have another slice of pizza, Del," Savannah said, setting one on her friend's plate as a diversion.

"*Is* it bad seeing Clint again?" Della persisted with a hint of orneriness.

"It's fine. No big deal," Savannah lied.

The truth was that she felt wonderful and awful at the same time. That her attraction to him was as potent as it had been when they were younger and that every glance at Clint, the sight of his every movement, the sound of his voice, being alone with him on her cousin's patio the previous evening, had only proven that to her.

"I never did understand what happened between the two of you," Della said. "I thought you were going to stick around. Marry him. That you and I would end up raising babies together right here."

Savannah exchanged a glance with her sister. Only Ivey knew the real story behind what had occurred fifteen years before. Ivey and their father, who had died two months after Savannah and Ivey had left town.

And as much as Savannah cared for Della, if she was going to tell anyone the truth about the events of the past, it would have to be Clint.

"Ivey and I just had our plans in order and decided to go through with them," Savannah said, as if there hadn't been anything more than that to their leaving Elk Creek. "You know we always talked about going as soon as we were both out of school."

"I know you talked about it before getting serious with Clint. But when you *did* get serious with Clint—and don't try to tell me now that you weren't because I *know* you were—I also know you were talking about marrying him and staying. I thought that's what would happen. But all of a sudden you just up and left, anyway.''

"More wine?" This from Savannah, another diversionary tactic.

It didn't work.

Della continued in spite of having her glass refilled. And in spite of having told Savannah this many times over the years in numerous attempts to persuade her to open up. "Poor Clint went wild when he heard you'd actually taken off. He'd been calling me, trying to figure out why you wouldn't see him or talk to him for those two weeks before, when you were playing hermit—for no reason I could understand, either. And then when you just left town...well, poor guy was beside himself. He thought I must have known what was going on, that you certainly would have confided in me, but what could I tell him? I didn't know any more than he did.''

"There wasn't anything else to know," Savannah lied again. "I made up my mind to go through with what Ivey and I had planned all along, and we left.''

It didn't take more than that to persuade Della that her curiosity was going to go unsatisfied yet again. Her curiosity about the past, at any rate. The present was something else again.

"So is there any chance for you and Clint getting together again, now that you're back?" Savannah's childhood friend asked.

"Getting together again? No," Savannah said, as if the very thought were ridiculous.

"Why not?"

"Clint and me together is ancient history.''

Kansas laughed out loud. "Not from the looks of

things last night. I don't think either of you were even aware that the rest of us were around the whole evening. And I saw you both out on the patio when I went into the kitchen for a glass of water—that barbecue scene did not look like ancient history.''

''Barbecue scene?'' Della and Ivey both parroted Kansas at once, their interest clearly piqued.

''We were just talking, and I happened to be sitting on the barbecue because all the furniture is away for the winter.''

''Hah! You were sitting on the barbecue because he lifted you up there,'' Kansas said with another laugh.

Eyebrows arched all around the coffee table.

Savannah made a face. ''My heel got caught on my hem. I nearly fell into the pit. Clint was just helping out.''

Everybody laughed at that, doing a chorus of ''Oh, sure'' and ''Yeah, right.''

''There's nothing going on between Clint and me,'' Savannah insisted. ''There's too much water under that bridge.''

''Really?'' Della said suspiciously. ''I thought you just left town because that's what you and Ivey had planned all along. That doesn't sound like too much water under the bridge.''

''I just meant that I went with Clint when we were kids. A whole lifetime ago. I'm a different person now—an adult. He's a different person now—''

''An *adult*,'' Ivey put in.

''Which makes you two *consenting* adults,'' Della added.

"And anything can happen between two consenting adults," Kansas finished.

Savannah rolled her eyes at the three of them. "Nothing is going to happen, because I won't let it," she said emphatically.

"Maybe you should," Ivey suggested.

"You know better than that," Savannah answered, giving her sister a meaningful look.

"Della's going to go away for a while and then come home to a fresh start. Your being here again could be the same thing for you and Clint—a fresh start," Kansas offered.

Della teared up once more. "Fresh starts aren't as easy as they sound," she said, obviously leaning more toward Savannah's side in that.

"But sometimes you have to make them, whether they're easy or not, and in the end they put a bright new spin on things," Ivey said.

Who could dispute that when both Ivey and Kansas were living proof of it?

But still neither Savannah nor Della seemed inclined to believe that any bright new spin might be in the offing for them.

"I think we ought to get back to work," Savannah said to change the subject.

This time it worked. Probably because the pizza was gone and everyone had slowed down on the wine. A general agreement went up, and they stood to clear the mess and head for Della's bedroom once more.

But as Savannah worked side by side with her sister and friends, Clint was still on her mind. Clint and fresh starts.

The trouble was, the past was there on her mind,

too. That part of the past that could never be forgotten. The part that meant the air between her and Clint wasn't clear.

And if the air wasn't clear between them, Savannah didn't think any kind of fresh start was possible.

Not that she wanted one.

Because she didn't.

Or so she told herself.

It was just that watching her sister so happy with Cully, and Kansas so happy with Linc, made it difficult to be alone. To keep resisting Clint's undeniable appeal. To keep resisting her own feelings for him—past and present.

Especially if he sought her out the way he had the night before. If he went on being as charming. As amusing. As handsome. As sexy...

And if he did? she asked herself. What was she going to do about it? Would she be able to keep resisting him, after all?

She was afraid she wouldn't be able to.

But she thought there might be one way to stop him from seeking her out. From being charming or amusing or wanting anything to do with her at all.

And that was to tell him the truth.

She just didn't know if she could do that, either.


It was nearly eleven o'clock when Savannah, Ivey, Della and Kansas called it a night. Kansas was staying over so Della wouldn't have to be alone.

As Ivey and Savannah were saying their goodbyes, Della apologized for the fact that she was going to leave town before Ivey and Cully's wedding and wouldn't be able to attend it. Ivey assured her she understood. Then the two Heller sisters headed out to Ivey's car.

But Ivey's car wasn't alone at the curb in front of the house. Behind it was parked a big white pickup truck, and sitting on the truck's hood—cowboy boot heels hooked on the bumper, elbows to wide-spread knees—were Cully and Clint.

"Hey, ladies," Cully called to them both, even though he only had eyes for Ivey.

Savannah's first thought was that this was some sort of setup her sister had devised. But Ivey seemed genuinely surprised as she made a beeline for her fiancé.

Savannah had no choice but to follow along. That or look like some kind of standoffish prig.

Not that there wasn't a part of her that didn't want to go over and say hello to Clint. After all, he looked incredible, sitting on the hood of that truck. Rugged. Relaxed. Full of the devil—if his one-sided grin at her was any indication.

He had on snug blue jeans and a red Henley T-shirt underneath a plaid flannel Western shirt that exposed the Henley at the collar. His sleeves were rolled to his elbows. Nothing flashy but still he looked great. So great that things that had been sleeping inside her woke up and stood at attention.

Savannah wandered along behind Ivey, feeling like a moth drawn to a flame, wondering as she did if her own jeans and purple turtleneck T-shirt were wilted after working in them all afternoon and evening.

"I brought Clint to see to Savannah gettin' home so we could have a moonlight drive in your car. Maybe test out the back seat," Cully said to Ivey.

Ivey glanced from Cully to Savannah, clearly unsure how Savannah would react to that suggestion.

Stepping into the breach, Clint spoke to Ivey but kept his gorgeous blue eyes on Savannah. "The truth is, I hog-tied him into this so he could lure you away and I could surprise Savannah with somethin'."

"Is that right?" Ivey pretended offense. "You had to be hog-tied to spend tonight with me?"

Cully hopped down, wrapped an arm around her waist and yanked her playfully to bang against his side. "What do you think?" he demanded in a voice full of innuendo.

Ivey giggled, butted him with her hip and then focused on Savannah again. "Do you mind if Cully and I go for a drive and Clint takes you home?"

Of course she minded. She was trying to steer clear of Clint.

Or at least one part of her was.

On the other hand, another part of her—that same part that had wanted to say hello to him—was shouting Yes! Yes! Yes! at the prospect of him taking her home.

"She minds," Clint answered before she could, giving her a sly look and another of those wicked grins. "But I'll make it worth her while."

"It's all settled, then," Cully said, trying to propel Ivey toward the other vehicle.

"Wait a minute," Ivey protested, not allowing herself to be moved from the spot. "Is this okay, Savannah?"

Savannah knew she should say it wasn't. That she should insist Ivey and Cully just drop her off on their way.

But there Clint stood, handsome, appealing, tossing her a wink that implied they shared something they didn't, and what she should do she couldn't.

"It's all right," she finally said, and was rewarded by a round of pleased grins.

Ivey and Cully said a fast good-night and nearly ran for Ivey's car, as if Savannah might change her mind if they hesitated. And Savannah was left standing on the sidewalk, facing Clint at a safe distance.

"But I'm really tired. It's late. I'd just like to go straight home," she informed him right off the bat, in an attempt to keep the time with him at a minimum. Better that than submit herself to too much of what she was worried she might not have the stamina to resist.

"I told you I have a surprise for you," he reminded.

"Well, give it to me quick so I can get home." Oh, but she'd sounded schoolmarmish! She hated that. And it was so unlike her. She never even used that tone of voice with her students.

"It isn't the kind of surprise I can hand over. It's a different kind of surprise," he said with a voice full of mystery, dangling keys in the air between them. "I have the keys to your heart."

"On a Bugs Bunny key ring?" she said with a little laugh in spite of herself.

He jiggled the keys once more but didn't offer any other explanation. He also didn't pay any attention to her reluctance. Instead he stood up on the bumper, jumped down and went to the passenger side of the truck to open the door for her.

He waited there like a valet until Savannah relented

and climbed into the truck. Then, with a satisfied grin even bigger than he'd given her before, he said, "Buckle up," closed the door and rounded the front of the truck on long, confident strides that caught Savannah's gaze and carried it along until he climbed into the other side of the cab.

"Have I got a treat for you," he said enticingly, starting the engine.

That was the last he said.

But the trip was a short one—a five-minute drive to Center Street, Elk Creek's main thoroughfare, the heart of the business district.

There were no lights on in any of the quaint buildings that lined Center Street. Most of them had been built years and years before in a variety of unfancy styles; one, two and three stories high. Different-colored paint and adornments like whitewashed shutters and special awnings distinguished one store or business from another, but everything was closed up tight for the night by then.

Not that that stopped Clint from pulling up to the curb—nose first—in front of Margie Wilson's Café.

Margie Wilson's Café had for years been the only sit-down restaurant in town—if the four booths at Dairy King didn't count. And now, one night a week, food prepared by Ally, Savannah's cousin Jackson's wife—who had been a chef in Denver—was served at Linc's honky-tonk, the Buckin' Bronco. But Margie Wilson's Café was still the main eatery.

Memories flooded through Savannah at the sight of the old diner, with its big picture window decorated with tied-back, ruffled curtains like an old-fashioned country kitchen.

Clint turned off the motor and got out of the truck, coming around to open Savannah's door.

"Does Margie know you swiped her keys?" she asked as she climbed down, assuming the keys he'd brandished were to the lock on the diner's door.

"I beg your pardon. I didn't *swipe* anything. I asked and she gave freely. Well, maybe not freely. I traded her a half cord of firewood for this privilege."

Clint led the way to the café's door and unlocked it. Once he'd pushed it open, he held an arm inside, motioning for her to go in ahead of him.

Savannah did, turning on the lights as she went. "What do you have up your sleeve?"

"Margie's homemade Peach Harvest Supreme."

Savannah knew her expression lit up at the mention of that. "Ice cream."

"Your favorite—unless that's changed. And the very last of the season. Now say you're sorry for thinkin' unkind thoughts about me tonight."

"For a bowl of Peach Harvest Supreme I'll say I'm sorry for thinking unkind thoughts for the past week."

"All of them about me?" he said in mock outrage.

None of her thoughts about him were unkind. Uncomfortable, maybe. But not unkind. "Just in general."

Clint closed and locked the door behind them, then went to the lunch counter.

Savannah followed him, trying not to notice how divinely he filled out the back pockets of his jeans with that taut, narrow, perfectly shaped derriere of his.

She hiked herself up onto one of the high stools attached to the counter and watched him go behind it to dish out the ice cream—giving her more than he took for himself and, indeed, finishing off the container.

"Looks like our positions are reversed here," he said as he slid her bowl in front of her and then leaned on the countertop to sample his own. "I used to think you were the most beautiful thing I'd ever seen when you were workin' back here."

"Must have been the lovely apron Margie made me wear."

"Or the smart lip you exchanged with ornery truck drivers who gave you a hard time," he added wryly.

"Are you saying I had an unpleasant disposition?" she asked, pretending offense.

"Now how could I be sayin' that when I was comin' in here orderin' up full meals I couldn't afford just so you'd have to wait on me?"

Savannah couldn't help smiling at that memory as she savored the delicacy she hadn't tasted in fifteen years. "I heard rumors that you were taking work doing any kind of odd jobs anybody wanted you to do to earn extra money to eat here," she teased.

"The Dairy King was more in line with my budget. A full four dollars for a plate of chicken-fried steak, mashed potatoes and gravy and biscuits—"

"Twice a day, sometimes."

"Twice a day, sometimes—was a big difference from a buck and a quarter for burger, fries and a giant malt over at the Dairy King."

"I think you asked me out on a date finally just to save yourself some money."

"And to get you alone," he confided with a rakish wiggle of his eyebrows and a flash of those alluring dimples.

Maybe it was the ice cream. Maybe it was this stroll down some of the only pleasant memories she had of her time here. Maybe it was being near enough to smell Clint's aftershave or the sound of his voice or the fact that the tension between them had once again dissolved and been replaced by a cozy, co-cooned feeling that seemed to have wrapped around them. But Savannah was at ease with him suddenly. And having a very good time.

She glanced around the restaurant. "I always liked it here. Margie mothered everybody who worked for her the way she mothered her own daughter, and it helped a little to fill the gap of not having a mom of my own."

"Margie's a good lady," Clint agreed.

"I was sorry that my uncle Shag didn't do right by her."

"The backdoor romance. She never let it show that he hurt her when he took up with Ally's mother in Denver—you did know that was the connection, didn't you?"

"Della told me that as far as anybody knows, Shag met Ally's mother after he turned the ranch over to Jackson and started spending more and more time in Colorado. Ally's mother wouldn't accept anything from him in the way of money or property, so he left part of everything to Ally. That's how Jackson and Ally got together."

"Right. I guess it was just in the cards for poor Margie to lose out so Jackson and Ally could hitch up down the road. It was fate," he said pointedly. "No telling how and when folks finally settle with who they're supposed to settle with. Or how they'll be brought together. Or when.''

"Mmm," Savannah agreed without committing to more than that. Then another positive recollection drifted into her mind. "I also always liked it when you'd come in and help on my nights to close," she said.

"What you liked was makin' me mop the floor."

Savannah laughed. "I'm no dummy."

"My payment for it eased the pain, though."

"I don't remember paying you."

"You don't remember kisses in the kitchen?"

A rush of warmth washed through her as those memories cropped up vividly enough to make her knees go weak.

"And kisses in the pantry," Clint continued. "And kisses in the meat locker. And kisses in the alley out back…''

"I should have worked you harder. I didn't know that was all payment for helping me around here," she joked, or attempted to, anyway. It came out in such a soft voice it sounded more seductive than she'd intended.

Clint opened his arms wide. "At your service. Anytime," he teased in return.

"For kisses or chores?" Where had *that* come from? She was flirting with him. And she hated herself for it.

"I'm available for either. Or both," he answered, making light of her question rather than pushing the way he might have.

"But are you available for taking me home?" she said suddenly, knowing she'd better stop this before she got carried away. And since they'd both finished their ice cream, ending the evening seemed like the safest route—if anything about Clint Culhane could be considered safe.

He didn't appear thrilled, but rather than argue the point, he set their bowls in the sink behind the counter, rinsed them and left them soaking as he came around to Savannah's side.

"There was a time when you'd have begged me *not* to take you home," he said as they headed for the door.

"Now my father isn't there waiting for me. And I never *begged*."

"Oh, I get it," Clint said, pretending indignation. "I was better than going home to a mean old man, but now I'm not better than going home to an empty house."

She laughed but didn't relent. "I'm sorry but I really am beat."

"Yeah, yeah, yeah. That's what they all say."

Savannah laughed at his rejected-suitor routine as he held the door open for her to go out. And she knew too well that it *was* only a routine. No man as terrific looking, as charismatic, as just plain nice as Clint was, experienced too much rejection from women.

Once he'd locked Margie Wilson's Café after them, he again held the truck's passenger door open for her, before going around to slide into the driver's side.

"So," he said as he backed away from the curb and headed north on Center Street. "I plied you with ice cream for a reason."

There seemed to be a note of reluctance in his voice

that made her think what was to come was not going
to be as enjoyable as what had just passed.

"What was the reason?"

"There are questions I need some answers to."

He said that amiably enough, and yet to Savannah
it had an ominous ring.

"You can ply me with ice cream and ask the questions, but that doesn't mean I'll give you the answers."

He glanced at her and smiled, dimpling up and easing some of the tension that had reemerged in her as
quickly as it had disappeared in the diner.

"How 'bout I ask 'em and you just think about
answerin' 'em—tomorrow, maybe?"

As strong as the part of her was that dreaded what
he might be about to ask, the other part of her that
kept urging her on tonight was thrilled by the prospect
of having a reason to see him the next day.

*I'm really losing my marbles,* she thought.

"I won't promise to give you answers to your questions tomorrow, either," she warned. But it came out
too flirtatiously to carry much weight.

"Okay. No promises. Except that you'll *think*
about givin' me some answers."

"I'll *think* about it. Maybe. After I hear the questions."

The distance out of Elk Creek to Savannah's house
was so short that they were already going up her drive
by then. Clint didn't say any more until he'd stopped
in front of the place and turned off the engine.

He pivoted in the seat, placing one muscled thigh
so that his knee was close to her and stretching his
right arm along the seat back.

He didn't touch her, but his hand was very near. Near enough that it wouldn't have taken more than a twitch for them to connect. And she was more aware of that than she wanted to be. More aware of a craving in herself for just that to happen.

"Well, here goes," he said as a segue. "Want me to just rattle 'em all off?"

Savannah shrugged, not intending to brush his hand with her shoulder, but doing it anyway before that shoulder went back into place. And even that small amount of contact left her having to tamp down the responding sparks erupting within her.

"I guess that's as good an idea as any," she said.

"I want to know why—out of the blue, fifteen years ago—you wouldn't see me or talk to me or answer the notes I sent you those last two weeks you were here. I want to know what happened to our talk about gettin' married, about you stayin' in Elk Creek, buildin' a life with me. I want to know why, when you did leave, you didn't so much as come to me, tell me you were goin' and say goodbye. I want to know what the hell went wrong just when I thought everything was goin' so right. Did I hurt you somehow? Did I say or do somethin' that drove you away? Did I take you for granted? What?"

He paused, and it seemed to Savannah that she could feel every furrow of his frown in her heart.

"Or did you just stop lovin' me?" he added quietly.

She'd expected that if this moment ever came it would be full of accusations and suspicions and well-deserved anger and outrage.

But none of that was there.

Instead he just sounded so confused. So baffled.
So hurt.

Even after all this time.

And it cut through her like a knife.

"I can tell you this much," she said very solemnly,
because even though he'd allowed her time to consider answering him—time she would take to consider it—she couldn't leave him thinking what he'd
apparently been thinking any longer. "I didn't leave
because of anything you said or did, or didn't say or
do. I didn't leave because I'd stopped…caring for
you."

She paused for a split second, debated about how
honest she should be at that moment and then blurted
out, "And leaving you was the hardest thing I've ever
done in my life."

Then she quickly opened the truck door and made
a run for her house, because she was afraid if she
didn't, she might not be able to keep from saying or
doing something before she'd fully thought it out.

Clint didn't just let her go, though. He caught up
with her on the porch, just as she was shakily using
her key.

"Savannah—"

"You gave me until tomorrow to think about answering your questions," she reminded him.

She could tell he was sorry he had. That he would
have liked to push for answers now.

But he held up a big hand—palm out—and said,
"Okay. I told you that, and I'll stick to it. If you'll
keep your word about considerin' givin' me some answers then."

"I'll think about it." And about *how* to tell him if she decided she could.

He smiled down at her, only slightly, but something inside her melted all over again. Especially when those crystal blue eyes of his caught and held hers.

"You never stopped carin', huh?" he said, teasing her, helping to lighten the moment once more.

"I didn't say 'never.' I said I didn't leave fifteen years ago because I'd stopped." But *never* was true, too, and somehow that was there in her voice, loud and clear. Heaven help her....

"Till tomorrow, then," he said.

"Tomorrow," she agreed, still captivated by his eyes when she should have rushed into the house to escape the spell they wove around her.

But she didn't rush into the house. She stayed right there on the porch. Looking up into his oh-so-handsome face as it drew nearer. Slowly, slowly nearer. Until he pressed his lips to hers in a gentle, tentative kiss that seemed to reclaim her in a small way.

And although the kiss was over almost before it had begun, and he was down the porch steps, back in his truck and pulling away from the house, she remained where she was, feeling the warm silk of his lips lingering on hers. Smelling his aftershave in her mind. Hearing his rich, masculine voice.

And deeply yearning for him to be there with her still; for time to be turned back.

Or maybe for the future to be as sweet as that one moment was.

As sweet as some of the past they'd shared.

# Chapter Four

Ordinarily Savannah could sleep until late in the morning without any problem. But she was wide-awake before dawn the next day. Still lying in bed, but wide-awake. Staring at the ceiling just as she had been most of the night. Thinking. About Clint. Again.

There was a lot to think about.

His questions.

Fresh starts.

Clearing the air.

The way he made her feel...

He was winning her over again, and she knew it.

He'd won her over when they were younger. When dating meant tempting her father's wrath. When no other boy had paid her much mind and she'd had too many problems at home and too many plans about how she could get away to bother with the opposite sex.

But Clint Culhane had broken through all those barriers. He'd introduced her to her own lighter side, shown her how to have fun.

Savannah had always been a strong person at the core. She'd had to be. After all, for as long as she could remember she'd been responsible for herself, for Ivey, for running interference for their father's foul disposition and tactlessness with everyone he encountered when he was alive. She'd always been the person other people leaned on.

Except with Clint.

Things with him had been different. He'd been an escape from the harshness of her father. From the all-work-and-no-play fierceness that had permeated life at home. He'd taught her how to have a good time. How to let go. How to forget everything else even for just a little while.

She'd been able to do all of that because Clint was there to take care of her for a change. To look out for her the way no one else ever had.

The previous evening with him at Margie Wilson's Café had brought that all back. He'd managed to get her to drop her guard. To relax and enjoy herself more thoroughly than she had since leaving Elk Creek and him behind. Since accepting the continuation of being the responsible one once she and Ivey were alone in the city.

She'd never found anybody but Clint who could make her actually feel carefree.

And it made him difficult to resist.

Especially when into the mix were other pleasures

in being with him. Pleasures like the way he looked, the way he smelled, the sound of his voice rolling over her like warm honey, the way it felt to have him touch her, kiss her...

But the air wasn't clear between them, she reminded herself.

And Della was right—fresh starts weren't so easy to come by.

*If* a fresh start was even what Savannah wanted. Which she didn't think she did.

*So answer his questions,* a little voice in the back of her mind goaded.

Because the answers to his questions were bound to change his attitude.

But somehow she didn't want to use them as that kind of weapon, to fend off his advances. She didn't want to use them as a weapon at all.

If she answered his questions it had to be for other reasons. It had to be to make him understand that he hadn't done anything wrong. That he wasn't to blame for her leaving Elk Creek.

He deserved to know that.

The blame for what had happened all those years ago was hers and hers alone. And she hated that he'd believed it was his. That wasn't fair. It wasn't something she'd even considered he might think, and now that she knew he did, how could she let it go on?

Sure, she'd told him nothing had been his fault, but without the truth to back up her statement, she'd seen in his face that he hadn't really accepted it. That he was still wondering what mistakes he'd made.

Which meant that she owed him the explanation

that would convince him he hadn't done anything wrong.

And if that explanation turned him cold in the process? If it kept him from pursuing her, from doing any more of the nice things he'd already done, from being as charming as he'd been, then it was probably all for the best.

*And if it cleared the air between them and opened the way for a fresh start?* that little voice asked.

A bubble of excitement rose up inside her at that possibility.

But she purposely popped it.

Clint might still be fun. He might be drop-dead gorgeous. And sexy. And an all-round great guy. And he might make her feel things she hadn't felt with anyone else.

But she'd been serious when she'd told her sister and her friends that there was too much water under the bridge between her and Clint.

Too much water and time and heartbreak and sadness and—

And still that bubble of excitement…of hope…rose up again, anyway.

One way or another, she had to tell him the whole story. Difficult as it might be.

And it would be difficult.

But she'd do it without letting herself entertain any thoughts that it might open the way for things to start up again for them in the future. She would explain what had happened, only because it seemed like the right thing to do. For his sake.

And after that?

It was anybody's guess what would happen after that.

But she steadfastly refused to hope that what happened after that would be something good.

When Savannah stepped out of the shower an hour later she heard breakfast-making sounds coming from the kitchen below, and she thought that Ivey must have come home hungry after spending the night at the Culhanes' place.

Savannah was glad for the company. Her sister would be a distraction from her own thoughts.

She towel dried her hair and brushed it, threw on a plain gray sweat suit and went downstairs.

But it wasn't Ivey she found in the kitchen.

It was Clint. Scrambling eggs. Frying bacon. Toasting bread.

Coffee was ready to be poured. The table was set for two, with a glass of orange juice at each place. And although he was dressed only for work, in well-worn jeans and a faded red Western shirt, he was a feast for her eyes that made her forget her stomach was empty.

"Oh. I thought you were Ivey," Savannah said, when he glanced at her over one shoulder.

Clint dimpled up for her with a warm smile and said, "'Mornin'."

Her heart did a little dance at that smile even as she felt herself tense up. She knew he'd come for the answers to his questions.

He'd told her he would give her until today to think about those answers, but she'd assumed he would call before coming over, arrange a time that gave her some warning, some chance to prepare. To dress better than she had and borrow some of Ivey's makeup again.

As it was, Savannah wasn't braced for it. Or crazy about the way she looked.

But she could hardly turn tail and run back upstairs for mascara, so she opted for toughing it out. At least she'd get this over and done with early.

"I talked Ivey out of her house key," he was saying. "Thought I'd come over, fix you breakfast before I get busy doing some work on the barn roof and the paddock fence." He winked at her. "In case you've forgotten, our agreement for rentin' your barn is that we don't let anything go to disrepair. Includin' you," he joked, raising his cooking fork.

Disrepair was just what she considered herself in, but it had nothing to do with a need for breakfast. It had to do with looking on the outside as if she could be headed for cleaning the barn and feeling on the inside as if her emotions were all in a jumble.

How could she be so glad to see the very person who was causing her such turmoil and costing her full nights of lost sleep?

Which reminded her that she probably had dark circles under her eyes, too, and didn't help matters any.

"Sit down," Clint suggested with a nod toward the table.

"Can I do something?"

"Pour coffee if you want."

She did, taking two cups with her to the table just as he slid eggs, bacon and toast onto plates and brought them with him to join her.

He set one plate in front of her and then sat across from her at the old metal kitchen table with the other.

"This is nice," she lied just to have something to say.

"I couldn't wait any longer to finally find out what went on that caused you to leave fifteen years ago," he said without preamble then. "I was wishin' I hadn't given you until today to think about it because it kept me on more pins and needles than I thought it would after all this time."

"I didn't guarantee I'd tell you. I just said I'd consider it," she reminded, uneasiness making her hedge.

He swallowed a bite of toast. "Did you consider it?"

"Mmm-hmm," she said around a mouthful of fluffy eggs that didn't want to pass through her tension-constricted throat.

"And?"

She washed the eggs down with a drink of orange juice and told herself to just get this over with. "And I decided to tell you the truth," she said, jumping in with both feet so she couldn't back out.

"Great. Let's hear it."

He said that with such high anticipation. With crystal blue eyes bright with curiosity. With that handsome, freshly shaven face as alight with eagerness as if he were going to have the solution to a deep mystery finally revealed to him.

Savannah had the sense that he expected what was about to come out to be something inconsequential. Something small. Something that amounted to a misunderstanding that they would both end up laughing over. Something that their immaturity had blown out of proportion.

But then he had no idea whatsoever what he was about to hear.

"Clint..."

Her voice alone was apparently enough to warn him because he stopped short, the fork midway to his mouth, and looked at her.

"This is a big deal," she cautioned.

A momentary frown pulled his eyebrows together. "Okay. Big deal, small deal—I don't care. Just tell me what the hell happened back then."

Just tell him what happened back then. It sounded so simple.

But it wasn't simple. Not for Savannah.

She tried to find the best way to begin. Failed. And opted for just saying it.

"I was pregnant."

Clint's fork had made it to his mouth and back to his plate by then, but he stopped chewing. Started again and swallowed as if he were having some trouble in that area now. On the plate the fork slipped out of his slackened hand as if he'd forgotten he even held it. His eyes never left her. And Savannah watched as shock, disbelief, then more shock raced across his face.

"Pregnant," he repeated. Not as quietly as she'd delivered the news, but almost. "We had a baby?"

Savannah shook her head. "I found out we were going to. I didn't know whether it was a good thing or a bad one. I was just stunned, I suppose. I never thought it would happen to me. I thought we'd been so careful...."

Too many years had passed to feel comfortable talking about intimacies they'd shared then, and so she stalled. Besides, she was rambling and she knew it.

She looked down at her nearly untouched plate of food, then back at Clint, forcing herself to go on more succinctly, just giving him the facts.

"I came home from the doctor's office. Ivey was here, upstairs. My father was outside. I went up to Ivey and told her. We were talking about it and we didn't hear Silas come in. Didn't hear him come upstairs. Didn't know he was eavesdropping on us."

Clint just went on staring at her from beneath a dark, troubled frown.

"Silas was madder than I'd ever seen him," she continued. "Furious. Enraged. He called me a whore. Said I was just like my whoring mother, but that at least she'd run off with that farm equipment salesman. I'd be right here for the whole town to see, embarrassing him even more than she had—"

"So you left to have our baby where it wouldn't embarrass him?" Clint guessed, sounding angry himself.

"No. It didn't get that far."

"He hit you" was the second guess, this one in a bitter tone.

"He never had before," she said, hating to sound as if she were defending her father, when she only intended to tell the truth.

Still, Clint took it as a defense and wouldn't accept it. "But he did everything short of that. He worked you and Ivey like dogs, deprived you of food if you did anything he didn't want you to do. He was abusive, Savannah. That's why I tried to talk you into getting out of this damn house. To get help in town for yourself and Ivey. Even to come to my folks—''

She didn't need reminding of any of that. She remembered it all too well. They were things she had refused to do, and that refusal to take any positive action before it was too late had left her feeling all the more at fault for what had happened. ''I was ashamed of the way he was. Of the way he treated us. I didn't want to air our dirty laundry in public,'' she said, sounding as feeble as she now thought the excuse to be.

''So he hit you,'' Clint repeated to spur her on.

''He slapped me. I didn't think he would, but he did. And when he did, I knew that I had to get away. I thought if I could get past him, get out of the house, I could run to you. But he caught me in the hall, not far from the steps. My running had only made him madder. He shook me so hard I thought my head was going to snap off. I yanked away from him but I was so dizzy...''

She had to pause to fight the tears that flooded her eyes even after all this time at just the memory of that day. ''He slapped me across the face again while I was still reeling. I lost my balance. I didn't realize how close I was to the stairs. I fell...''

''Down the steps?''

''All the way down the whole flight.''

''You lost the baby,'' he said very, very softly.

''That night.''

Clint's jaw clenched. He raised his chin. Studied the pot of geraniums hanging above the kitchen window. And let silence fall.

Savannah couldn't tell what was going on in his mind. But she could see that whatever it was, it was stormy.

Then he dipped his chin and looked at her once more. "You let that damn, mean old man know about our baby before you told me?"

There was a shade of anger in his tone again. But it was nowhere near as much anger as she'd felt for herself since that hated day.

"Not on purpose. Never on purpose would I have told him before you. I just didn't know he'd come back inside."

"You should have come to see me before you even told Ivey. Before you told anybody. Before you ever came near this place carrying our baby. You should have come to me so we could have handled it together. So we could have eloped. So we could have done anything but have you face that old bastard alone."

How could she answer that? It was all part of that "water under the bridge."

"Hindsight is twenty-twenty," she said softly.

Clint shook his head, and she watched so many emotions rush through his expression—confusion, pain, rage. "Of all the things I've thought over the years, I never imagined anything like this."

"I know. But I didn't realize you would believe you'd driven me away, either. I thought you would just figure I'd made good on my plans with Ivey to leave Elk Creek. After last night, hearing all your questions, I didn't want you to go on assuming it was something you did."

"It *was* something I did. I got you pregnant."

Savannah didn't have a response to that either, except to say, "It's all in the past."

"And you didn't tell me even after the fact," he said, clearly unhappy about that. "You just cut yourself off from me completely those last two weeks before you left town."

"I was upset, confused. Grieving, I guess. I knew for sure, then, that I had to get as far away from that man as I could. I knew I had to get my sister away and that if I saw you, talked to you, I wouldn't be able to do it. And if I didn't go, neither would Ivey."

Savannah hesitated because the rest was even more difficult to admit. But in almost a whisper, she managed. "Besides, I couldn't face you, Clint. I couldn't look you in the eye and tell you I'd lost our baby. That I'd let my father kill it. That I hadn't protected it...." She swallowed back the rise of misery in her throat.

She wasn't going to cry! She wasn't!

She blinked back tears fiercely, trained her gaze on that same geranium pot that had caught Clint's eye moments before and went on as best she could. "Besides, I knew you hated my father. I worried, too, that you might go after him. That you might do something and end up getting hurt yourself. Or into terrible trouble. It just seemed like the best thing for me to do was to keep quiet about everything and leave."

Neither of them said anything for a while.

Savannah went from looking at the geraniums to staring at her nearly untouched plate of food, giving Clint time to absorb everything.

But he still sounded as if he was on overload, as if he was stunned and working to grasp all she'd finally told him when he muttered, "My God. A baby."

Then, as if the idea struck him like a thunderbolt, he said, "Were you okay physically? Was there permanent damage?"

"No, no permanent damage." Not physical, anyway.

"But you must have been hurt? Sick?"

"I had bruises from his hands, from the slap, that's all."

"That's all," he echoed facetiously. "And what about the miscarriage? How bad was that?"

"There was cramping, bleeding…" That suddenly seemed too personal to talk about and so she let her voice dwindle off. "But everything healed." Except maybe her heart.

"I never thought…" His voice dwindled off, too.

"I guess now you have a lot to think about."

"A baby," he said yet again, as if repeating it might help it seem real. "We could have had a baby.…"

She wished he would stop saying it, because every time he did it was like a slap. But she tried not to let her pain show. She just sat there, stone still, straight-backed, suffering it, staring again at the plate of cold food in front of her.

Just then Ivey and Cully came through the back door. To Savannah their voices seemed loud in the silence that had settled around her and Clint. Loud and happy and lighthearted.

"You 'bout ready to go to work?" Cully asked Clint.

Savannah looked from her sister and future brother-in-law to Clint. He seemed dazed. His brow was wrinkled forlornly, and she had the impression that he didn't know what to do from there.

After a moment he said, "Yeah. Sure," still sounding as if he were part zombie.

He shot one glance—one frown—at Savannah, but without saying anything to her he stood and followed his brother through the mudroom and out the door Ivey and Cully had just come in.

Savannah could feel her sister's confused eyes on her. She only vaguely heard Ivey ask what was the matter.

But she couldn't answer her. Couldn't say anything at all while she was fighting so hard not to cry.

*That's that,* she thought. *Now he knows.*

And it had definitely changed his attitude.

Which would no doubt keep Clint as far away from her as he could get.

The trouble was, that didn't make her happy or relieved or any of the things she told herself she should have been. Instead it added to the sadness that had lingered around the edges of her life for so long now.

Added to it. Made it well up inside her.

And the sadness threatened to overwhelm her.


"What will you do? Hide in the house until the wedding? Wear blinders through the ceremony and then run back to Cheyenne rather than face Clint again?"

"Sounds like a plan to me," Savannah agreed, even though Ivey was only being facetious.

Ally, the wife of their cousin Jackson, was cooking

up something special at Linc's honky-tonk that night in honor of Ivey and Cully. All the Culhanes and all the Hellers would be at the Buckin' Bronco. Which meant Clint would be there. And because of that, Savannah was dragging her feet about going. Much the way she'd dragged her feet about seeing him at Ivey's engagement dinner.

Okay, so it was cowardly, and being cowardly went against her grain. But she and Clint hadn't spoken since that morning, when she'd told him about her pregnancy so many years ago. He hadn't come anywhere near the house all day, had barely glanced toward it and hadn't so much as smiled or waved in her direction to acknowledge that he'd seen her at the window when she thought he had.

Instead, the two times their eyes had met through the glass, he'd only beetled up his brow as if one glimpse of her was troubling. And then he'd looked away. Both times.

He'd just looked away....

"He doesn't want to see me. I don't want to see him. It's better if I don't go," Savannah said, sitting on the edge of her mattress rather than getting ready for the evening ahead, watching Ivey slip her feet into the shoes that finished her outfit.

They were in their old childhood bedroom, still a spartan space even with the addition of suitcases and the portable television Ivey had brought from their apartment in Cheyenne.

Besides the TV, there were two small twin-size beds, the table between them and a four-drawer bureau. Period. No scrap of wallpaper, nothing more than a plain shade for a window covering, no decoration of any kind. Now, just as it had been all the time they'd inhabited it growing up, it looked more like a cell than a bedroom.

"There will be a lot of people there," Ivey said, trying to persuade Savannah. "The place is always packed. You won't have to go near Clint if you don't want to."

But that was the point. She would want to, just the way she'd wanted to all along—against her better judgment. And chances were he wouldn't want to be in the same room with her. That he couldn't stand to be around her anymore.

And she didn't think she could bear watching that. Watching him turn away and walk out rather than share the same space, rather than breathe the same air she did.

"You go. Have a good time. I'll be fine here," Savannah urged.

"Well, I won't be fine if you're here. I want you with us. Besides, it isn't as if you and Clint are a couple who's just had a fight or broken up or something. You said yourself you didn't tell him the truth expecting that it would lead to anything."

"It isn't that I expected it to lead to anything. I didn't *want* it to lead to anything. But I didn't think he'd end up hating me, either. Or at least I hoped he wouldn't," she added in a quieter voice.

"He doesn't hate you."

"Call it what you want, but it sure looked to me like he hated the sight of me so much he had to turn his head when he saw me the rest of the day."

"He was busy. You aren't even sure he *did* see you today. From inside the house it might have only

seemed like he saw you at the window. Maybe he
didn't.''

Savannah didn't say anything to that. She didn't
have to. Ivey's feeble, unconvinced tone of voice said
it all.

"What you told him is a lot to swallow in one
lump, Savannah,'' Ivey went on to compensate.
"You've had fifteen years to sit with it, and we both
know it still bothers you, that it can still get you
down. It had to be the only thing he thought about
today, and so he was distracted and trying to accept
it all. Or he really might not have seen you in the
window.

"But I'll say the same thing I did about the engagement dinner—you're going to have to be in the
same vicinity he is sooner or later, so why not sooner?
Why not tonight, with a whole slew of other people
around, too? Why not get it over with? It'll give you
a good indication of whether he's honestly going to
steer clear of you over this or if he's just trying to
grasp it all before he goes on, and the two of you can
still end up friends.''

Friends.

Just friends.

Why did it make her heart clench up to think the
best they could ever be was just friends? What else
did she expect? What else did she want?

She couldn't answer that, even though it was her
own question. She just didn't know what she wanted.

She knew only that since he'd walked out of the
kitchen she'd had a knot the size of Texas in her
stomach. She'd spent the day reminding herself that
she hadn't told Clint the truth about the baby just

because it might clear the air and offer them a fresh start. She'd reminded herself that there was nothing between the two of them now. That there never would be in the future. And that no matter what his reaction, it didn't change anything. It didn't matter.

Except that it did matter. It had mattered a whole lot every time she'd glanced out the window and been drawn to watching him work. It had mattered every time she'd wished she was out there with him. Or that he was inside with her. It had mattered a whole lot when she thought he'd caught sight of her and turned his head....

"Come on. I want you to be there tonight," Ivey said. "You know Clint. It isn't as if he'll make some sort of scene or something. The worst that can happen is that he'll stay away from you and you'll stay away from him—which is what you've been trying to do since you came back to Elk Creek, anyway. Just come and get past seeing him for the first time now that he knows the truth. It's not going to get any easier if you wait and eventually have to be in the same place at the same time." Ivey paused and then said, "You know I'm right."

"Okay. You're right."

"Then you'll go."

That knot in Savannah's stomach got even bigger and tighter. But she finally conceded. "I suppose. But if it gets ugly—"

"It isn't going to get ugly. We're talking about Clint Culhane, not Silas Heller. It won't get ugly."

Maybe not.

But how much would it hurt if he turned cold, accusing, hatred-filled eyes on her? If contempt twisted his handsome face? If he could barely be civil to her, instead of his usual charming, teasing, incorrigible self?

It would hurt terribly.

But in a way Savannah felt as if it was no more than she had coming. And Ivey was on the mark when she said it would be better to find out if that was how things were going to be from here on.

"Let's get you dressed," her sister suggested, heading for the closet.

But Savannah didn't care what she wore.

Her heart just wasn't in the evening to come.

In fact, she was almost as enthusiastic as someone dressing to attend their own hanging.

Before being turned into a honky-tonk, the Buckin' Bronco had been a holding barn for cattle being transported by train to market. In its new incarnation it looked like an Old West saloon.

A huge, carved-walnut bar took up one end; tables filled the space in front of it for about a third of the length of the place, and a dance floor stretched to the foot of a raised stage.

Ivey hadn't been kidding about the Buckin' Bronco being packed. As Savannah followed her sister and Cully in from the open great doors she had to dodge bodies and chairs and dancers and waiters and waitresses to get to the large round table that was being held for their party.

The Heller cousins were already at the table. All but Ally, who was in the kitchen preparing the lemon-pepper chicken breasts, fettuccine Alfredo, stuffed eggplant and rosemary focaccia that was coming out in large quantities to satisfy hungry customers.

Cully had picked up both Ivey and Savannah, but he hadn't said anything about whether or not Clint was coming. Or about any of what Savannah had revealed to his brother that morning, although she assumed Clint must have told Cully and Yance.

She couldn't help thinking that it was a bad sign that Clint hadn't come along with Cully to get them. Had he felt kindly toward her—the way he had the previous evening—he would have shown up, too.

Maybe he wouldn't come at all, she thought. Maybe knowing she'd be there would keep him away.

But no sooner had that crossed her mind than Clint and Yance appeared in the great doors, scanning the crowd to locate their table.

"Over here!" Jackson called with a loud whistle and a wave of his arms.

Savannah froze in the chair she'd just been seated in, her eyes glued to Clint as he wove a similar path through the crowded room.

He had on jeans, darker blue than the work-faded ones of earlier, and a crisp yellow shirt. His hair was combed in that haphazard way of his. His handsome face was clean shaven. And although he wasn't what anyone would consider dressed up, to Savannah he looked wonderful.

Not as wonderful as if he'd actually glanced her way and smiled, but wonderful just the same.

Heartbreakingly wonderful.

But then maybe the overwhelming feeling that he'd turned against her once and for all was what was making her heart break.

She didn't want to be caught staring at him, so she tried to pretend she hadn't noticed him and brushed a nonexistent speck off the long sleeve of the navy blue jumpsuit she'd worn for the occasion. Then she tugged at the high neck, feeling a little as if she needed some kind of armor for the moment when Clint reached the table.

And then that moment was upon her.

Greetings went up all the way around, making it not too obvious that Savannah only muttered a general hello.

She let herself steal a small peek at Clint as he took a chair far on the other side of the enormous table. He glanced at her at the same instant, but only briefly, before averting his eyes.

And that set the course for the evening.

All through dinner. All through dessert and drinks and dancing afterward, they were like two strangers who only talked to the people in the group they each encountered separately.

Clearly whatever had been going on between them in the past couple of days was no longer happening because, unlike the other times they'd been together, tonight Clint didn't even watch her surreptitiously. He didn't snatch glimpses of her out of the corner of his eye. He barely looked at her when courtesy demanded it. And she had the sense that he was doing his best to forget she even existed.

Maybe they didn't really know each other, Savannah thought as the evening stretched on that way. Because the Clint of long ago would have forgiven her anything.

But then she had to admit that he could be thinking

that the Savannah he thought he knew from long ago would have *told* him anything.

At least there wasn't a scene. No reprisals. No outward repercussions, and that was something to be grateful for, she told herself. It was good that they'd be able to go through nights like tonight and the rest of the wedding preparations and celebrations they'd both have to attend without being overtly unpleasant. Being civil, albeit coolly, remotely civil. Removed from each other as much as possible.

But it sapped any fun out of the evening for her. Even though she reminded herself that she wasn't in Elk Creek to be with Clint. To have fun with Clint.

But as the hour approached eleven and Savannah was hoping the evening was nearing its end, something changed.

Clint started to study her as if she were a bug under a microscope. Staring at her openly, pensively—if the frown that creased his brow was any indication.

That went on for what seemed like an eternity to Savannah, who was having some trouble not squirming, before he stood and came around the table to hold out a hand to her.

"How 'bout takin' a walk with me?" he asked in a very solemn voice.

Savannah didn't think twice about it. She was so relieved just to have him speaking to her that she slipped her hand into his much bigger, warmer one and let him lead her out of the honky-tonk.

Neither of them said anything as they stepped into the cool October air or as they wandered across the road to the old, pale yellow Victorian train depot with its white gingerbread trim.

The depot was dark except for a single light above the barred ticket window that was closed for the night. But that didn't seem to make any difference to Clint as he took Savannah up the six steps to the planked platform, protected from the weather by a roof on spindled poles.

He went all the way to the bench that faced the tracks before releasing her hand and going himself to lean a broad shoulder against one of the posts. He crossed his arms over his chest, his right ankle over his left and again settled his gaze on her.

No more comfortable beneath his scrutiny now than she had been inside the Buckin' Bronco, Savannah sat on the bench, not knowing what to do or say. Her back was ramrod straight. She felt as if she were about to be taken to task and was ready to face it without cowering—the way she'd faced reprimands from her father without showing fear.

After a few moments like that, Clint said, "I'm still tryin' to let it all sink in."

He didn't have to tell her what he meant. "I know it's a shock," she said, referring to what she'd told him that morning as if the whole day and evening hadn't passed since they'd last talked about it.

"It's a *big* shock," he agreed. "And strange to feel the things I'm feelin' when it all happened so long ago. Almost seems as if it just happened fresh."

Savannah nodded, understanding that to him it was fresh.

"I don't know," he said out of the blue, shaking his head, looking up at the whitewashed ceiling above them. "Things keep rolling through my mind. Through me. I couldn't even tell Cully or Yance—it all just seems so damn strange. Strange that it ever happened. Strange that I didn't know. Strange that it can be so powerful this far down the road.''

"I'm sure," she muttered for lack of anything better to say, wondering if he'd just brought her out there to talk about his confusion or if there was more to it than that. Maybe he'd taken her away to rake her over the coals in private.

He sighed, shook his head again and leveled penetrating eyes on her. "But I'll tell you what keeps comin' back to me," he said.

*Here we go,* she thought, bracing for the worst.

"In the whole fifteen years since you left I haven't ever stopped havin' feelin's for you, Savannah. And what I'm wonderin' is if maybe we shouldn't try puttin' the past behind us."

For a moment she wasn't sure she was hearing him correctly. Not when she'd been expecting so much worse. Then what he'd said registered.

It wasn't exactly clear air or the proposal of a fresh start, but it still made bright, shiny things go off inside her. Bright, shiny things she tried to ignore as the other, saner part of her warned that she was treading very near the exact territory she'd come to Elk Creek intending to avoid.

"*Can* you put the past behind you?" she asked, because she wasn't so sure she could. Especially when she hadn't been able to so far.

"I don't know," he repeated. "But I know I'd like to try. Your reason for leavin' so long ago was different from what I've thought all this time. Better in some ways—you didn't go because you'd stopped carin' for me, or because I'd ruined somethin' be-

tween us. You left for reasons that didn't have anything to do with us or what we had together. So I just
keep thinkin' that maybe that makes it worth testin'
the line to see if what we had might still be there.''

"And how would we do that?''

He smiled with only one side of his mouth. A small
smile, but a smile nonetheless, as if he might have
been worried she wouldn't entertain the possibility at
all and was pleased that she hadn't turned him down
cold.

"We could start by puttin' your schoolteachin' experience to good use,'' he said. "You could go with
me tomorrow night to help decorate the gym for the
homecoming dance. Maybe we could go to the game.
Then the dance. And there's the weddin'. We could
just spend some time gettin' to know each other
again. Seein' where it goes—if it goes anywhere.''

"And all while you're trying to come to grips
with...what happened before?''

He nodded almost imperceptibly. "Unless, of
course, you don't have any of those old feelin's left,
can't stand the sight of me and would rather go on
the way you have been—tryin' to pretend I'm not
right there in front of you.''

"Seemed like that's what you were doing tonight.''

He laughed only slightly, but it was enough to
lighten the tension swirling around them. "I was. But
it didn't work. I still couldn't remember that there was
anybody in the place but you and me.''

"And what happens if we find out the feelings
aren't the same? Or that they are but there are just
too many things in the past that we can't put behind
us?''

"Then I guess we'll go our separate ways again," he said softly, as if that thought was painful for him to entertain.

Or maybe that was how it seemed to Savannah because just his saying it was like a knife jabbed into her heart.

"What do you say?" he asked then.

What could she say when that heartache was there to let her know she didn't just want to go her separate way—at least not without exploring the feelings she had for him?

"Decorate the gym. Go to the football game and maybe the dance," she reiterated, thinking that it all sounded innocent enough. What harm could there be in things as simple as those? "Okay. I guess it couldn't hurt anything." Too much.

But as she sat there, watching him across the small gap between them, seeing the way the dim light christened his rugged features, wanting to go to him, to feel his arms wrap around her, to have him pull her close against the hardness of his body, she wondered how she could help but be hurt if she ended up having to leave him behind a second time.

A little afraid of thoughts like that and what they might mean, she stood suddenly and nodded in the direction of the Buckin' Bronco. "But for now we should get back before somebody comes looking for us."

Clint didn't balk at the idea. Instead he shrugged away from the spindled pole as if he was satisfied that he'd gotten what he'd set out for and didn't want to rock the boat by pushing for anything else right at that moment.

He crossed the distance to her on two long strides that echoed on the hollow station platform floor and held his hand out to her the same way he had in the honky-tonk. Only this time Savannah hesitated.

She knew how good it would feel—how good it had felt—to have her own smaller hand encased in his powerful, callused one. And it was no mean feat to let go once it was there. Or to resist the other urges running rampant through her.

But in the end it was resistance she was short of, and she took his hand for the second time that night.

He didn't just take it and lead her across the street, though. He pulled her closer to him, almost up against his chest, and searched her face as if relearning it, letting his gaze caress her.

"Welcome home," he said very softly.

Then he dipped his head down to press his mouth against hers in a warm, honeyed kiss that did, indeed, welcome her home, but with some reservations that she wished weren't there. Not when she was yearning for him to hold her closer. For him to wrap his arms around her tightly. For him to kiss her more passionately....

But none of that happened.

Instead the kiss stayed soft, chaste, sweet—nowhere near what she would have liked it to be.

And it didn't last long before he ended it.

He took her back to the Buckin' Bronco, where a whole slew of friends and relatives carried her away for toasts to Ivey and Cully before everyone ended the evening and said good-night.

It didn't seem to matter that she didn't get another chance to talk to Clint.

Because no amount of distractions could keep her from focusing on him as surely as if they'd been by themselves.

And nothing could keep her from wondering what would happen when they were....

## Chapter Five

"Sneak attack from the back!"

Yance's warning was just enough louder than a whisper to alert Clint to what was coming. Which, Clint knew, was his older brother's purpose. It was a signal that Yance was ready for him to take over with their nieces.

Clint and Yance were minding Cully's two little girls the next afternoon while Cully tended to some wedding details. Clint was mending a fence that surrounded a field not far from the main Culhane house, and Yance had had Amy and Randa with him in the barn for more than an hour. Now it was Clint's turn.

Quiet little-girl giggles would have warned him of the coming onslaught, anyway, because Amy and Randa couldn't suppress them as they ran up to him from behind. Amy—who was slightly taller because she was a year older than three-year-old Randa—took a flying leap from a hay bale nearby and sprang onto his back. Randa only grabbed him around the knees and hung on like a big hug.

"We gotcha! We gotcha!" was Amy's victory cry as both girls' giggles pealed out in full force now.

"Must be time for cookies and milk," Clint said in response.

"Yeah! Yeah! I want some." Randa again.

"Me, too!"

Clint reached an arm around his back and slid Amy to his hip. Then he scooped Randa up with his free arm and carried the small bundles of dungarees, flannel shirts and unruly mop-top hair toward the house they all shared.

"Isn't Uncle Yance comin'?" Randa asked, seeing her other uncle headed to the barn again.

Yance heard the question and waved without turning around.

"He must have more work to do," Clint said simply, himself glad for the break.

The Culhane kitchen was a large affair in the rear of the house. A great big country kitchen that hadn't seen much actual cooking since the three brothers had taken over the homestead from their parents. Still, it was an inviting room with birch cupboards, a white tile floor, white marble countertops and dated appliances—all but the microwave oven and the refrigerator, which was restaurant-size to accommodate the three men and two kids.

Clint took a carton of milk from the refrigerator, grabbed a package of chocolate chip cookies and three glasses and joined his nieces at the breakfast bar that divided the large space in half—work space on one side, expansive rectangular oak table and chairs on the other.

The girls had already climbed onto the bar stools on the eating side of the bar, so Clint stationed himself opposite them, poured milk, ripped open the cookie package, and the three of them dug in without ceremony.

"Can I dunk my cookies in your milk?" Randa asked him after taking a drink of hers that left her with a milk mustache.

"What's wrong with dunkin' your cookies in your own milk?" Clint asked.

"She doesn't like to drink it after there's crumbs in it," Amy supplied, apparently having no qualms about that herself because she was happily dipping and munching.

"Is that why?" Clint asked the younger girl.

"Yes-it-is," Randa said so fast the words ran together and became one.

Clint laughed and passed his glass over.

"Thank-you-very-much," his smallest niece said, once more without a space between the words.

It was a new thing with Randa, and no one had figured out the origin. It drove Cully crazy, but it only made Clint smile.

He took a cookie for himself and reached across to dunk it in his glass, too, as Amy and Randa began to chatter about the coming wedding of their father and Ivey, their new dresses for the occasion and being flower girls—things they'd been talking about nonstop since preparations had started.

Clint tried to pay attention, but he'd heard it all at

least a dozen times already, and he couldn't keep his mind from wandering even as his eyes remained on his nieces.

Would his and Savannah's baby have been a boy or a girl? The thought drifted through his mind as he watched the two little imps before him.

It was no easy thing absorbing the news that he and Savannah had created a child together. Although he'd been trying hard to, since Savannah had told him the previous day.

*A baby,* he kept thinking.

A baby...

But whether or not it had been a boy or a girl, it wouldn't be a baby now. Or even a child as young as Amy or Randa. It would be a teenager. Fourteen years old.

And that was even harder to grasp.

Him, a father to a fourteen-year-old? He couldn't fathom what that might be like.

But he did know what it was like to have a couple of young kids around—kids the age of Amy and Randa—because he and Yance both pitched in with the girls. And he also knew he enjoyed it.

Clint was crazy about the two tiny beauties who faced him, chatting away a mile a minute. And he'd long thought how much he'd like having a couple of kids of his own.

That made it all the tougher to learn now that there had been one. A long time ago. A child of his making, who hadn't been allowed a life because some heavy-handed jackass hadn't been able to control his temper.

Just the thought made Clint's blood boil.

Silas Heller had essentially killed that baby. His own grandchild.

Clint's child.

Clint and Savannah's child.

And gotten away with it....

Damn, but Clint wished that old SOB was still around. Maybe if he was—if Clint could confront him, have this out with him—he'd feel better.

But he doubted it.

He didn't think anything would make him feel better about this.

If only Savannah had come straight from the doctor's office to him, he couldn't help thinking. If only she hadn't told anyone until she'd seen him....

Sure, it would have been a shock. It would have made waves—unexpected pregnancies between two people, barely more than kids themselves and who weren't married, would have definitely been an eyebrow raiser and a gossip inducer around Elk Creek.

But Clint would have taken the heat. He would have been glad for the impetus to marry Savannah.

Real glad.

Because the whole time they'd talked about her staying, about getting married, he'd known she was torn between doing that and the plan she and Ivey had for leaving town and their cranky old cuss of a father when Ivey graduated from high school.

Clint had been afraid he might lose Savannah to that plan. He'd hoped he could talk her out of it. Hoped she'd loved him enough to cancel it, even if it did mean Ivey might end up staying, too. But he'd known that Savannah had felt so responsible for Ivey.

Still, if he'd known about the baby...

Could he have persuaded Savannah to stay and marry him?

He thought he could have. In fact, he was sure he could have. That that would have been what tipped the scales in his favor.

And then they would have been a family. All this time.

There'd have been more kids.

He and Savannah would have been man and wife. Mom and Dad. They'd have had the life they'd day-dreamed out loud about having.

If only she'd come to him first....

The cookie he was holding suddenly crumbled beneath the tightening force of his fingers.

Clint hadn't realized the effect these thoughts were having on him until that moment. Then he became aware of the rigidity of his jaw. That his teeth were clenched. That one hand was in a fist while the other had crushed the cookie.

"Are you mad at me, Uncle Clint? I didn't dropped it in your milk on purpose," Randa was saying.

The tone of his niece's voice penetrated his musings, and when he focused on the two little girls across from him he could see that they were watching him the way they did when they'd done something they thought they were about to get into trouble for.

It was clear that not only were his thoughts affecting his teeth, jaw and hands, but apparently his expression had gotten pretty intimidating, too. Intimidating enough to quiet the girls' chatter and make them leery of what was to come.

He closed his eyes for a moment, forced his features to relax and then opened his eyes once more.

"No, I'm not mad at you, sweetheart," he assured his niece, proving it by handing her another cookie to replace the one she'd apparently lost in his glass.

But was he mad in general? he asked himself.

To tell the truth, he didn't know what he was.

At any given moment he was mad. Or hurt. Or resentful. Or sad. Or melancholy. Or a whole world of other things as the news of that baby, as thoughts of how things might have been, went through his mind.

But he couldn't pinpoint any one definitive way he felt about any of it. He just didn't know how he felt about something that had happened so long ago.

How *should* he feel about something that could have changed the whole course of his life if it hadn't been so prematurely ended? Something that, long ago or not, had just struck a blow to him now and left an injury as real as if it had occurred yesterday?

And what about his feelings for Savannah? he asked himself.

He didn't have a clear answer to that, either.

There was only one thing he knew with any certainty: he wasn't any less attracted to her.

This whole thing might have been easier if he was.

But just wondering about how he felt about her was all it took to send an image flashing through his mind of the natural beauty that haunted his days and nights. Of how her hair looked better after only one toss of her head than most women's looked fresh out of the beauty parlor. Of those lavender eyes. Of damned cute freckles. Of that body his was craving like a suffocating man craved air.

No, he wasn't any less attracted to her.

But he did have some hard feelings about what had gone on fifteen years ago.

He wasn't exactly sure whether those hard feelings were aimed at Savannah. Or at her father. Or at fate. Or maybe at everything rolled up together.

What he was sure of, though, was that just that mental image of her was enough to relax his jaw and unclench his teeth and hands. It was enough to make him certain that he wanted some time with her just the way he'd suggested the previous evening.

He wanted to get to know her again. Get to know the woman she'd grown up to be. He wanted to bring all the feelings he'd had for her for the better part of his life to the surface again, check them out, see if there was any substance to them. He wanted to know if he really could put the past behind them. And if there was a reason to look to the future.

Maybe what he would find out was that those new, hard feelings about the baby they'd lost couldn't be shed.

Maybe he'd find out that those old feelings he'd harbored for Savannah all this time were like dust in a trunk—scattered into nothing when the lid was taken off them and a little fresh air blew in.

Or maybe he'd find out that the past didn't have much bearing on the present or the future and that he and Savannah really were meant to be together. That nothing—not lost babies or years apart—could change that.

But one way or another he was going to get some answers to the questions that had replaced those Savannah had answered about what had driven her out of town fifteen years ago.

And he was going to do it with Savannah right there beside him. Across a table from him. Within reaching distance....

Which, for some reason that defied logic or common sense or sanity, made what sounded like it would be a hard journey seem more like a pleasure cruise.

Savannah felt like a teenager herself as she stood at the living room window waiting for Clint to pick her up that evening. Nervous and excited. Jittery and impatient. Apprehensive and eager.

She'd probably decorated a hundred gymnasiums for teenage dances and sock hops and award ceremonies and celebrations since becoming a junior high school teacher. She volunteered more than anyone else at her school.

She enjoyed it. Enjoyed working with the kids in a fun, relaxed atmosphere that put everyone on a level unlike the student-teacher relationship of the classroom. It also fulfilled a part of her that regretted having missed out on those experiences in her own teen years. Her father hadn't permitted either Savannah or Ivey to "waste time on such stupid, worthless things," and as a result neither of his daughters had attended a single dance growing up, let alone taken hours away from work at home to help decorate for them.

Savannah hadn't connected with Clint until the last week of their senior year, so even that opportunity had presented itself too late, although she'd always wondered what it might have been like to have hooked up with him earlier and had him include her in the preparations and then taken her to an actual dance.

Now, it seemed, she was about to find out, and that's what had her stomach all ajumble, adrenaline pumping through her veins and high anticipation almost a living, breathing being inside her.

She worried, as well, that things might not be quite the same between them, now that he knew about the baby. But she didn't have time to ponder that because just then she saw Clint's truck turn up the drive.

He was five minutes early, and she took that as a good sign. If he had reservations about this seeing-if-they-could-put-the-past-behind-them proposition, he probably wouldn't have been ahead of schedule. Dragging his feet would have been more likely.

Not that she was convinced she was interested in putting the past behind them so they could explore the possibilities of the future. But, hey, she was here in Elk Creek, a handsome guy wanted to show her a good time, and that was nice.

At least that's how she was trying to look at this.

She backed away from the window before he could see that she'd been watching for him. With her mind on other things, she slipped her hands under the long, dark purple turtleneck tunic sweater she had on and searched in vain for pockets to put them in. But the black leggings didn't have pockets, and she was left without a nonchalant pose as she answered Clint's knock on the door.

So instead, she opened it and hung on to the edge.

"Hi," she greeted.

"Hi, yourself," he said with a smile she thought might be slightly tentative.

But otherwise he looked great in age-softened jeans and a pale blue Henley T-shirt that made Savannah's mouth go dry.

Actually the shirt itself didn't accomplish that, but it hugged his super-flat belly and his broad, hard chest and shoulders like a second skin. The sleeves stretched across bulging biceps and were pushed up to his elbows to expose thick, powerful forearms and wrists that she had an inordinately vivid memory of…and fondness for. Plus it brought out the color of his eyes. Altogether it made for a strikingly attractive, masculine vision, and that was what hit her with the force of an eighteen-wheeler.

"Ready to go?" he asked, after giving her a quick once-over and broadening his smile as if he liked what he saw.

Savannah took a breath to calm herself down and said, "Sure. Do I need to bring anything?"

"Just you. What else would you bring?"

She shrugged. "Guess I'm just used to running things like this and having to make sure we've got what we need. I feel naked going empty-handed."

"Don't tease me now," he joked, holding open the screen to let her out.

Savannah called goodbye to Ivey, who was in the kitchen, and pulled the door closed behind her.

Clint had never let her get into a car or truck without opening the door for her, and he didn't now. Afterward he rounded the front end and she marveled at his attractiveness, indulging herself like a dieter with an ice-cream cone—savoring the sight of him before averting her eyes, so he wouldn't catch her at it.

"So how does a bachelor without any kids get roped into decorating the gym for the homecoming dance?" she asked as he headed down the drive.

"I used to be the assistant coach of the football team. A few years back John Dorsey—remember John Dorsey?"

"Big guy. Quarterback. Went to college on an athletic scholarship, wouldn't take so much as a sip of beer to save his life, so it was everybody's goal to corrupt him?"

"That's the one. After college he came back here to teach and coach, been here ever since. Anyway, he couldn't get a parent to volunteer to help with the team. He and I were pretty good friends. He asked me to do it, and since I could spare the time I did it. For four years. Then he found a father who was willing to help out, and I had more on my hands with the ranch, so I stopped. But along the way I'd also pitched in on the decorations for the dances—me and a lot of the parents and a lot of other folk who just do it for the heck of it. Somehow I've kept at it. You know we old codgers stay away from the prom and the sweetheart dance and the other socials, but homecoming gets a full turnout of alumni."

"No, I didn't know that. How would I, when I never went to one?"

"That's right. I forgot about your father not letting you go to even school functions."

"But I get to go to this year's," she reminded him when reference to her father seemed to sober his expression considerably.

But not for long. Apparently her unintentional and only slightly flirtatious tone had an immediate effect, because Clint cast her a glance, gave her a wink and said, "You mean I'll be takin' you to your very first Elk Creek High homecoming?"

"My very first," she confirmed.

Which was probably only fitting since he'd been her first in so many other things. First and only in some. Mainly because he was such a hard act to follow....

They'd arrived at the school by then—a three-story, redbrick building where classes for elementary school-age children were held on the ground floor, junior high on the second and senior on the third. The parking lot was already dotted with cars and trucks, newer models that likely belonged to the adults, and older, much more beat-up vehicles that Savannah assumed belonged to the kids who were helping, too.

"Here we are," Clint announced needlessly as he turned off the engine.

Again he came around to her side. She might not have waited for him, except she was paying more attention to her study of the old school building than to getting out of the truck.

"Looks the same," she commented.

"It is the same. All but for the new carpet, new paint and a display case in the lobby."

There was something comforting in knowing that the school had stayed the way it had been all that time ago, when Savannah had been a student there.

She'd always liked school. She and Ivey might not have fit in very well in the boy's clothes their father made them wear and with their hair cropped short the way he'd forced them to keep it, but school had still been where they could go to get away from the irascible Silas. It had been where they could go to find some peace, some fairness and more care than their father had ever shown them. Not to mention that schoolwork had been a far sight easier than the back-breaking ranch work Silas heaped on them at home in his quest to deny they were girls and turn them into the boys he'd rather have had.

After crossing the school yard from the parking lot, Savannah and Clint went through the double doors in the front of the building, spent a few minutes at the trophy case, so Savannah could look at the sports and academic awards displayed there and then took a sharp left turn into the gymnasium.

Adults and teenagers alike were already at work stringing crepe paper from the rafters, blowing up balloons and making ornamental flowers in the school colors—silver and red.

Warm hellos greeted them as they went in, and Savannah realized it didn't take much to be welcomed back into the embrace of the small town. She'd already renewed some old acquaintances at the funeral services for Bucky Dennehy and met the few new people who'd moved into town, but even without any kind of lengthy reunions she was still being included in overtures as openly friendly as if she hadn't taken a fifteen-year hiatus from Elk Creek.

Just inside the gym doors Clint took her arm and leaned in close to her ear. "I had 'em keep one job in particular open for you," he confided.

Something hot and honeyed sluiced all through her from just that touch of his hand on her arm and the feel of his breath against her ear, and it took Savannah a moment to let his words sink in.

When they had, she said, "And what job would that be? Cleaning the bathrooms for the big night?"

"Nah, I don't want you havin' *that* much fun. You won't have to get your hands wet with this."

Still holding her arm he guided her to a folding table near the end wall, where one of the basketball hoop backboards had been raised up to free the painted cinder block expanse.

"You get to do the before-and-after we have planned this year," Clint announced once they were there. "Thought you might get a kick out of seein' how everybody's changed. Or hasn't."

Savannah wasn't sure what he meant until she spotted the stacks of photographs on the folding table. All in sets of twos, they were yearbook pictures paper-clipped to more recent shots of a number of Elk Creek High's alumni.

"Oh, my gosh, is that really Linc?" Savannah said, picking up the pair that depicted her cousin and taking a closer look at the old photo.

"That's him," Clint confirmed. "Funny to see 'em, isn't it? That's why I thought you'd enjoy it."

"Where's yours?"

"In there somewhere. Along with yours."

"Mine? I didn't have a picture in the yearbook. My father wouldn't pay to have one taken, and I hardly wanted that bowl-cut hairdo he made me wear captured on film for eternity."

"Got one, anyway. Of you and of Ivey," he said, sounding pleased with himself.

"You didn't," Savannah challenged as she searched through the pictures until she came across an old album photo of herself and Ivey as small children. It had been taken on her cousins' back patio near the swimming pool.

"Linc, Beth or Jackson had to have given you this," she said with a laugh at the sight of herself and her sister—two skinny moppets of probably eight and ten.

"We never reveal our sources."

"And what about current pictures? You can't have any of those," she said even as she removed the paper clip and took from behind the old snapshot both her own and Ivey's most recent teacher photos.

"And Ivey did this," she said, laughing at the conspiracy that had apparently been going on behind her back.

Clint took the snapshot and Savannah's newer picture, comparing them side by side. "Big improvement. *Big* improvement."

"It's a good thing."

He set the photographs on the table again. "So what do you say? Think you can handle this?"

"You aren't going to help?" she asked, feeling let down at the prospect of losing his company.

"As soon as I crank that other basketball hoop up out of the way. Can you handle this till I come back?"

So long as she knew he was coming back her spirits rose again. "I think I can manage. But don't be gone too long—in case some of these pictures get separated and I can't tell who's who."

"Count on it," he assured, giving her arm a little squeeze before releasing it.

The letdown feeling returned at losing his touch but

it helped that that parting squeeze set off more of the hot and honeyed something to do battle with it.

*Just an old friend showing you a nice time. That's all Clint is. That's all this is,* she reminded herself.

But her rationalizing didn't do much to counteract what he'd set off in her. Maybe concentrating on something else would help, she thought, and went to work taping the before-and-after pictures to the wall.

But as she proceeded she found that the vaguely familiar faces couldn't hold her attention. Her eyes kept straying to Clint, all the way across the gym, working to raise the backboard.

And for some reason, rather than appreciating the sight of hard muscles swelling to crank the old-fashioned equipment out of the way, Savannah began to worry again.

Was it possible for him not to be bitter about the past? she wondered.

So far she hadn't seen any signs of resentment in him. But as she snatched glances in his direction she caught him keeping an eye on two teenage boys not far away from where he was. Two teenage boys who were probably fourteen or fifteen.

Clint seemed to study them as if they were a new life form he'd just discovered, all the while with a very serious expression on his handsome face, as if something about what he saw disturbed him.

But the boys weren't doing anything but setting up a refreshment area. There was nothing about that to bother Clint. He could only be thinking about the baby that would have been roughly the same age as those boys if it had been allowed to be born. The baby that might have been his son.

And in that moment Savannah had a sudden flash of knowledge that putting the past behind them wasn't going to be uncomplicated. That maybe it really wouldn't be possible at all.

*If it isn't, it isn't,* her more pragmatic side said.

But her emotional side wasn't quite so flippant about it.

There was something between her and Clint that she couldn't ignore. Some indefinable, but incredibly potent, chemistry, and the thought that maybe this getting to know each other again and trying to forget the past wouldn't pan out caused Savannah a pang somewhere near her heart.

But there was nothing she could do about it, that voice of reason said. Either they were meant to be or they weren't. And only time would tell one way or another.

So the best thing she could do, she decided, was just what she'd set out for tonight—have a little fun with the man who had taught her how to do that in the first place so many years ago.

And if nothing else came of it but that they ended up knowing for sure that there couldn't be anything between them now, then at least maybe they could meet at family gatherings with Ivey and Cully without wondering what might have been if only they'd given it a second try.

But somehow, in a quiet corner of her heart, she couldn't help hoping that that wasn't how things would turn out.

Savannah and Clint were the last of the volunteers left in the gym when the decorating was finished.

They were sitting on the floor with their backs against the folded-up bleachers, where everyone had dropped to have a final cookie and soda pop someone had brought as rewards for a job well done.

But it was late and everyone else had said good-night and gone home, while Savannah and Clint lingered, side by side, surveying what they'd accomplished.

"So how many times tonight were you asked if you were married?" Clint asked, leaning his head against the bleachers so he could look at her.

Apparently he was settling in for a while just when Savannah expected him to suggest that they leave, too. Not that she wanted to go. She was so tired she just wanted to sit there, so relaxed her inhibitions and concerns were all subdued. And she felt she hadn't had enough time alone with Clint yet and was in no hurry to exert the energy to move at all, let alone to end the evening.

"Let's see," she said as if she were counting the are-you-married questions in her mind. "Only about three hundred and twenty times."

"I think a couple of those guys who asked were more than just curious. I think they were interested for themselves. I was beginning to wonder if I'd have to take Mitch Hayes outside."

"Wasn't he the nerdish guy with the perpetual tape on his glasses who was a year ahead of us in school?"

"The one and only. He got contact lenses and thinks it turned him into Casanova."

"He does look better than he did."

"Interested?"

"Should I be?"

"I don't think so," he answered, enunciating each word slowly and with mock menace. Then his wonderfully chiseled features eased into another smile. "So here's *my* marriage question for you—how come?"

"How come I'm not married?"

"And never have been."

It was her turn to flash him a frown that didn't have any substance. "Are you fishing for compliments?"

"Is there one in this?"

"Don't sound so surprised."

"Okay, now I want the explanation for sure. Why haven't you ever married?"

"I think it has something to do with expecting other people to live up to—"

"Me?" he said hopefully.

"To live up to your first love," she amended.

"Which was me," he pointed out with satisfaction. "I must have been pretty good," he added with a wiggle of one eyebrow that said his smugness was nothing more than part of the running joke they were engaged in.

"Let's just say those adolescent feelings were pretty strong, and I've been waiting to experience something that matches up."

He grinned at her, deepening his dimples into grooves. "It's okay. I won't get a swelled head if you just say 'I haven't found anybody I was as crazy wild in love with as I was crazy wild in love with you.'"

"Oh, wouldn't you just love for me to say *that!*" she countered.

"Why yes, ma'am, I would," he confessed with a

laugh. "Are you at least tellin' me that you never even got close to marryin' anybody else?"

She considered lying but there was a blunt streak in Savannah that spurred her to say, "No, I never did. I've dated a few guys for long periods of time, but it's never turned into anything more. I like my work and—"

"We've already established that you turned into a workaholic."

"And so far I haven't come across anybody who makes me want to change that."

"Till now—say that," he instructed.

She was enjoying talking to him so much she didn't mind the slightly probing vein in his jests.

"What hat size did you say you wear now?"

"Same as always."

"As I recall you and your brothers and my cousins Linc and Jackson were all known for being rowdy, hell-raising, heartbreakers who could get any girl you wanted." And who were notoriously handsome, but she didn't include that. "Nowhere was there any mention of self-effacing humbleness. Guess that hasn't changed."

"When you got it, flaunt it?"

"You're asking me?"

"I was hoping it was a good excuse."

They both laughed at that.

None of the Culhanes—or her cousins for that matter—lacked confidence or a healthy male ego, but neither were any of them arrogant or conceited, so there was no seriousness to this. It was all in fun.

And it was fun. Savannah was having a good time. But just then the janitor cut it short by poking his head into the gym to ask if he could close up for the night.

Clint told him they were thinking about sleeping there, but if he was going to insist, they'd get out.

The janitor—the same janitor who'd been there when they were students and looked as old as Methuselah—said he had to insist, so Clint stood, offering Savannah a hand to hoist her to her feet, too.

"I'm afraid we're being evicted," he said as he did.

*Too bad,* was what she thought but she only accepted his help up.

On the way back to her place the flirting was at a minimum as they talked about who had changed the most and who hadn't from the pictures Savannah had put up on the gymnasium wall. Then there they were, on her porch once again to say good-night.

Savannah unlocked and opened the front door but stayed outside, debating with herself about asking him in. But in the end she decided that in the interest of this being only the beginning of the new getting-to-know-each-other phase she should treat it like a first date. And she wouldn't ask a first date in.

Clint faced her a foot or so away, his weight slung on one hip, his hands in his pockets, thumbs pointing at the zipper of his jeans—something she wished she wasn't so aware of—and said, "That wasn't too bad, was it?"

"Tonight? Not too bad, no," she said in understatement when it fact she was sorry to have it over with.

"You know, when I plotted this course for us and roped you into decoratin' the gym and going to the game and the dance I forgot about the pregame rally tomorrow night. There'll be a big bonfire, fireworks, the whole shebang. I was plannin' to add my voice to the noise but I'd sure have a better time if you'd go with me.''

Savannah couldn't help smiling at the charm of the man. Somehow he managed to make that sound aw-shucksish, and at the same time there was a wickedly delicious glimmer in his eyes.

''What if I say no?'' she said just to be ornery.

''You'll be ruinin' my whole evenin'. And maybe I'll just come on over here and do some rallyin' to make you give in, anyway.''

''Will you bring fireworks?''

''I might make some of my own.'' He took a step nearer, closing even just the scant distance between them so that Savannah had to tip her head far back to look up at him.

''Then again,'' he added, ''if it's fireworks you want, I might be able to light some right now.''

Cocky. There was the most alluringly cocky arch to just one of his eyebrows.

''Is that so?'' Savannah said with a tilt of her chin to answer his cockiness with a touch of her own.

''Do you doubt me?''

''For all I know you could be way out of practice in the lighting fireworks department.''

Okay, so she was dancing too near the flames by saying things like that. But she couldn't help herself.

''Is that a challenge?'' he asked, easing nearer still. In fact he was so close they were mere inches apart and she could feel the heat of his big body.

''A challenge? No, just an observation.''

"You're sayin' I look out of practice?"

"It's all right," she said, pretending to console him. "I told you, I know how hard it is to have overly high expectations after your first love. When they aren't met time and again you give up trying and just concentrate on other things. No wonder your ranch keeps growing."

He knew that for what it was—her goading him because even though she'd admitted as much to him, he'd yet to admit it to her.

And he didn't now. He only played along with the banter.

"I'm gonna have to prove you wrong about my being out of practice, you know," he warned, reaching up to fiddle with a strand of her hair where it hung loosely around her shoulders.

"You don't *have* to," she said, getting cold feet suddenly.

He just smiled, a softer, Cheshire cat sort of smile, as his face began a slow descent and his hand found its way into her hair, to cup the back of her head.

Butterflies took flight in Savannah's stomach as surely as if this really were her first date, her first kiss, and all the while a cautioning voice in her mind chanted, *You shouldn't be doing this...you shouldn't be doing this.*

But it didn't matter.

She angled her chin upward more than it already was and relaxed her mouth, and when his lips touched hers she was ready and waiting. Eager to have his clean breath mingling with hers; to smell the scent of his aftershave; to feel the scant brush of his rougher skin along her cheek, her chin; to know again the smooth, adept expertise of that supple, sensuous mouth of his....

Sure, he'd kissed her the night before—and the night before that—but not like this.

Those other kisses had been more reserved, more chaste.

But this was a real kiss. A deep kiss that was shot through with a sense of reconnecting. That left no doubts that he was a man and she was a woman, and that there were, indeed, fireworks between them.

Savannah only had one complaint about it.

He ended it much, much sooner than she wanted him to. So much sooner that it took her a moment to realize he wasn't just changing positions, that he'd actually stopped.

In a voice husky enough to make it clear that the impact of that kiss wasn't on her alone, he said, "I don't know about you, but I'm seein' sparks."

"You're not supposed to admit that," she whispered in response, almost as if speaking too loudly might cost her the memory of his lips on hers.

Clint only smiled down at her, no cockiness in his expression or his attitude now. "Will you go with me to the rally tomorrow night?" he asked then, probably because he thought her defenses were down.

And they were.

"It would be a shame to miss it," she muttered.

Clint's smile broadened into a grin. "I'll be here at seven."

She nodded, wishing hard for another kiss. For another and a lot more to go along with it. For kisses that not only met and matched those that had been her first, but that were better than any that had come since.

But he didn't kiss her again.

He slid his hand out of her hair and stepped back. "See you then," he said.

Savannah only nodded and watched him cross the porch, go down the stairs with a little hop to his step and get into the truck again.

But that single kiss had been enough to let her know that her feelings for Clint were coming to life once more, regardless of whether or not it was wise. Regardless of whether or not they were just starting out again and didn't have any idea where this might all end up.

She was a little scared, because she really didn't know if things between them were going to work out.

But she was also filled with something else. Something delicious and delightful and warm and wonderful. Something that left her tingling all over and most definitely craving more—more kisses, more than kisses, more of Clint.

And as she watched him drive away with a wave of one of those big hands, she couldn't deny that nothing in the last fifteen years had even come close to competing with that first love and all that went with it.

And that, quite possibly, nothing ever would....

## Chapter Six

For Savannah, being back in the house where she'd grown up was strange. It was less strange when Ivey or someone else was there. But she was alone the next afternoon as she tried to work on her master's thesis.

Her sister was baby-sitting Amy and Randa Culhane for the day and had taken them out for a long walk. None of the Culhane brothers were tending to anything in or around the barn. Neither the clock radio nor the small portable television was on. And in the silence that was left, memories kept visiting at odd moments for no real reason Savannah could put her finger on.

No matter where in the house she moved to, the sense of her father's presence kept following her. From her bedroom to the desk in the alcove off the living room, and even now where she sat at the kitchen table.

It was almost as if the ghost of Silas Heller had come to haunt her—that's how vivid was her sense of him. She'd write a sentence or two, and then her mind wouldn't be anywhere near sixteenth-century poets. Instead she'd be listening for sounds of her father the way she had as a kid when she'd tried to avoid him if she could.

That had been easier said than done. The man seemed to have been everywhere, like some demon in a horror movie, showing up just when she thought she'd dodged him, in the unlikeliest places.

Or lurking outside a door to eavesdrop and then bringing down his wrath upon her when he didn't like what he heard....

Not that his wrath had ever involved hitting either her or Ivey until that fateful day fifteen years ago. But Clint had been right in saying that previously Silas had abused them verbally and psychologically by working them like dogs and doling out punishments that didn't fit their minor infractions.

But it was that fateful day fifteen years ago that kept replaying itself in her mind when she was trying to write.

The events.

The outcome.

The "if onlys"...

If only she hadn't gone home after that doctor's appointment.

If only she hadn't told Ivey when they were anywhere near the house or Silas.

If only she'd gone straight to Clint.

If only she'd kept herself out of her father's reach....

"We're back."

Savannah jumped a foot off her chair at the sound of Ivey's voice calling from the dining room. She'd been so lost in her own thoughts that she hadn't heard the front door open or anyone come in.

Her heart was still racing when Ivey stepped into the kitchen with Amy and Randa following right behind. Randa skipped into the room, to the chair across from Savannah to sit down while Amy took a more leisurely stroll.

"We're gonna have a tea party," Randa announced.

"I thought you were working upstairs," Ivey said as if it went with the little girl's statement.

"I couldn't concentrate."

"We can go have our tea party at the Culhanes' house if our being here will bother you."

"No, that's okay. I'm not getting anything done and a tea party sounds nice. Maybe a break will do me some good." Plus she was glad for the company to chase away what the silence had brought her. "That is, if I'm invited," she added.

"We'll invited you," Randa offered.

Amy joined Savannah and Randa at the table while Ivey set out cookies and made tea—very weak tea that was mostly milk for the two kids. In the meantime the girls filled Savannah in on the specifics of their walk.

When they'd exhausted that subject, Amy pointed at Savannah's books and notepads where they still lay open in front of her.

"What're you doin' with all that stuff?"

"Schoolwork," Savannah said simply as Ivey sat beside her and they all sweetened their tea and chose cookies.

"Are you a teacher like Ivey is?" Randa again.

"I teach older kids than Ivey does, but yes, I'm a teacher, too."

"Are you married?" Amy asked, her voice tinged with a touch of romantic awe at the possibility.

Savannah laughed at both the child's tone and the fact that even one of Elk Creek's youngest citizens was asking her that question. "No, I'm not married."

"Uncle Clint likes you, though, I think," Amy said as if there was consolation in that.

"Do you have somes kids of your own?" Randa asked around a mouthful of cookies, sitting very straight and prim, as if playing grown-up for the occasion of their tea party.

Savannah was grateful for the diversion from Amy's comment about Clint even though it lit a tiny spark in her to hear it. "No, I don't have any children of my own," she said, feeling that old familiar stab she suffered every time someone posed that question to her.

"You should have some kids," Amy chimed in. "Ivey didn't have no kids but now she'll have us. And you should have some, too."

"You think so, huh?" Savannah said with a slight chuckle at the finality of the four-year-old's declaration.

"Don't you like kids?" Randa asked, as if it would be tragic if she didn't.

"I like kids a lot."

"Don't you want somes?"

Savannah shrugged her shoulders. "Oh, I don't know. I think about it."

"Then why don't you get some?"

"Maybe I wouldn't be a very good mother."

The words slipped out on their own, as naturally as if it wasn't a secret sentiment she'd guarded for most of her adult life.

She hoped Ivey might overlook it, accept it as a simple, meaningless part of a simple, meaningless conversation with these two tiny girls.

But there must have been something in her tone that told Ivey that wasn't the case. That gave it away as the truth Savannah had thought for the past fifteen years, even if she hadn't ever voiced it.

"What? Are you kidding?" Ivey said a little belatedly, as if it had taken her a few moments to get over the shock of having heard something she couldn't believe. "*You* not a good mother?"

Savannah waved her hand as if shooing a gnat, hoping that might put her sister off the track.

But it didn't.

"You mean that, don't you?" Ivey said, as if she could suddenly see clearly what had been right there in front of her face all this time. "You don't think you'd make a good mother, even after taking care of me for as long as I can remember. Even though you're great with kids. Even though you've won Teacher of the Year three times. You still honestly think you might not be a good mother."

"Mothers protect their children from harm."

Savannah hadn't meant for that to come out, either, and would have taken the words back if she could have. She'd have taken this whole conversation back if she could have.

What had gotten into her? For fifteen years she'd kept these thoughts to herself, and now here they were sneaking out.

It was this place, she decided. And the vivid memory of their father. It was as if his harsh judgment of her was spurring her to admit the worst of her own feelings about herself.

"Oh, Savannah," Ivey groaned compassionately. "How could you think such a crazy thing? Is it being here again that caused these thoughts or have you always had them?"

"No big deal," Savannah said as if her sister were making a much larger issue out of this than it was.

But Ivey still wasn't fooled.

"I'll bet that's why you aren't getting any work done today, isn't it? You've been reliving the past and beating yourself up all over again, haven't you?"

It was useless for Savannah to deny the facts, so the best she could hope for was to minimize them. "The walls seem to be talking today, is all."

"The walls *talk?*" Amy asked, intrigued. "I want to hear!"

"Me, too!" Randa chimed in. "What do they say? Do they say 'Feed me, feed me,' like Amy's doll does?"

Savannah managed a laugh at that, glad for the diversion presented by the two little imps. She reached across the table and gently tickled Randa's side. "The walls don't really talk. That's just a saying."

"What's it mean?" this from Amy.

Ivey answered her but her words were aimed more

pointedly for Savannah. "It means Savannah was having too many memories of things that happened here a long, *long* time ago. And they're making her think things she shouldn't be thinking."

"Are there pi'tures of stuff what happened here a long, *long* time ago on the walls?" Randa asked, clearly still confused.

"No, no pictures," Savannah assured.

"Did somebody *write* on the walls? 'Cuz me 'n' Randa got in lots of trouble for writin' on the walls in our room with our new colors."

"No, no writing, either," Savannah answered again, this time gathering up her books and papers into a pile. "But I think maybe I'd better go upstairs and see if I can't do some writing on paper, now that you guys have helped get my mind off those other things."

"Except that we haven't," Ivey said under her breath.

"Sure you have," Savannah answered, forcing herself to sound much more cheerful than she felt.

"You know," Ivey said seriously, "I'd rather you don't stay for the wedding if being here makes you go through all this again."

"It's okay, Ivey. It's no big deal," Savannah repeated. "This place just got to me a little today is all. Don't worry about it."

Ivey still didn't look convinced, but Savannah didn't want to talk any more about any of this. Or think any more about it. And maybe now that the house wasn't empty she could get something accomplished on her thesis before the day was completely wasted.

"We're goin' to the rally-thingy tonight. Are you?" Amy asked Savannah as Savannah picked up her things to escape.

"I am. I'm going with your uncle Clint." And wasn't that a nice reminder to help alleviate her other, darker musings of the day.

"We'll see you there, then," Randa added. "Dress in your warm clothes—it's gettin' cold outside, and Ivey says it looks like maybe it'll snow!"

"I'll remember," Savannah said with a laugh. "See you guys tonight."

The little girls said goodbye and wasted no time going on to the subject of the rally and what a rally actually was.

But Savannah didn't hear Ivey adding to the conversation.

Instead she could feel her sister's eyes following her out of the room and she had no doubt that had she turned and looked back she'd have found Ivey's expression full of concern.

But there was no call for that concern.

Savannah might have voiced some of what she'd carried around inside her for fifteen years, some of what she'd never said even to Ivey before, about her feelings that she might not be the kind of woman who should ever become a mother. But it didn't change anything.

The bottom line was that whether she talked about it or not, whether Ivey or anyone else told her she was mistaken, she'd allowed harm to come to her and Clint's baby.

She'd lived with that fact of life. She'd go on living with it.

It was her burden to carry.

And no one needed to deal with that except her.

A light snow had begun to fall by dusk that evening, and anticipation of being with Clint again helped Savannah evade the dark thoughts and feelings that had shadowed her throughout the day.

She took a shower just after the soup and sandwich supper she and Ivey shared, washed her hair and even let her sister paint her nails with clear polish. Then she borrowed some of Ivey's mascara and a faint dusting of her blush, applied a hint of lip gloss and turned her attention to dressing.

Along with the snow, the temperature had dropped considerably, so she opted for heavy tan-colored slacks and a cable-knit sweater over a high-necked blouse with a bit of lace around the edge. She brushed her hair, caught it in an elastic ruffle only inches short of the long ends so it draped back loosely, and deemed herself ready at just about the time two trucks paraded up the drive. Culhanes in tandem.

Ivey was already waiting downstairs by then and had gone out and gotten into Cully's truck when Savannah made it to the foot of the stairs.

Clint was in the entryway. He had on black corduroy Western-cut jeans that hugged his hips and thighs with a caress Savannah's own hands itched to bestow, and a blindingly white turtleneck T-shirt under a black jean jacket that made him look rough and rugged and spruced up all at once.

And just that simple sight of him was enough to make her stomach flutter, her mouth go dry and her entire body shift into alert.

"You don't *look* like you had a bad day," he said in greeting. His gaze went from top to toe and back again, what he saw causing an appreciative arch to one eyebrow.

"Who says I had a bad day?"

"Ivey. On her way out. She said, 'Be nice to Savannah, she's had a bad day.'"

Savannah wished her sister were still there so she could kick her. "My day was fine. Frustrating because I tried to work and didn't get much accomplished, but fine."

He held up both hands, big palms outward in surrender. "I believe you. I believe you," he said in response to the somewhat hard edge in her voice.

But the hard edge wasn't intended for Clint, it was a reaction to Ivey's no-doubt-well-intentioned but out-of-line comment, so Savannah forced a small laugh and apologized. "I'm sorry. I didn't mean to jump down your throat. Maybe I didn't have the greatest day."

"Guess we'll have to put some extra effort into improvin' things tonight then."

It wouldn't take any extra effort. Her day was vastly improved just by having him standing there, tall, muscular, so handsome it made her knees weak, and smiling at her with those supple lips that she kept imagining him using to kiss her hello. Smiling at her, too, with those gorgeous crystal blue eyes of his that could replace the furnace for the heat they were emitting in her direction.

"We'd better go," she said, because that's just what she didn't want to do. Because what she did want to do was stay right there, alone with him, and she was afraid if she didn't hurry their departure, she might suggest that they never leave at all.

"They won't wait for us, that's for sure," he agreed.

He held the screen open for her, and as she passed in front of him to go out she caught a whiff of his aftershave—a cool, clean scent that made her think of ocean breezes and clear water—and fought the urge to stand on tiptoe and indulge in a few moments of the pure pleasure of breathing him in.

"So how was your day?" she asked instead, after he'd closed up her house and they were on their way to his truck.

"Fine. Yance and Cully and I brought in a small herd from one of the far pastures—none too soon from the looks of things," he added with a glance skyward at the snowflakes drifting down around them. Then he opened her side of the truck, handed her in and as soon as she was sitting on the cab seat, confided, "But it went too slow since I was champin' at the bit to get over here to you tonight."

He said that with an edge of exaggeration to it that made her laugh genuinely this time. "Don't shovel it on too thick. We can't roll down the windows."

He only winked outrageously at her, closed the door and rounded the truck to get in behind the wheel.

"Ivey isn't the only one who thinks you had a bad day," he said as he headed for town. "Tonight at dinner, Amy and Randa told us you looked sad this afternoon."

"Geez, I didn't think I was *that* much of a downer today."

"Amy and Randa talk nonstop about anything and

everything—in case you hadn't noticed yet,'' he said. But then he went on, anyway. ''They said somethin' about you feelin' bad because you couldn't be a mother.''

Oh, great. From the mouths of babes...

''What I said when they asked was that I didn't have any kids, so I didn't know if I'd be a *good* mother or not,'' she paraphrased to camouflage the real exchange at the tea party.

Clint glanced at her from the corner of his eye, assessing her again. Though this time what he was assessing didn't seem to be her appearance. ''I think you'd be a pretty good mother.''

''That was the general consensus arrived at today, too.''

Apparently he noticed that curt tone to her voice again. ''Sore point,'' Clint guessed, saying it more to himself than to her.

''Let's talk about something else.''

He smiled lopsidedly, his expression full of mischief. ''How 'bout this weather we're havin', and don't you just look fetchin' as all get-out tonight? Is that better?''

''Fetching?'' she repeated to tease him, laughing once more.

''Would you like *handsome* better?''

''Handsome? Makes me sound like a big, horsey woman.''

''How 'bout, you're a feast for these old eyes?''

''*Old* eyes? We're the same age. I think I'd have to take offense to that.''

He gave her a full-beam, dimpled grin and said,

"Sweetheart, I could look at you all day and all night
and still not get my fill. How's that?"

"Good. That one's good." And even though they
were only joking with each other it made her feel a
whole lot better than she had since getting out of bed
this morning.

But then that was something Clint always could
accomplish.

The rally was at the school and when Savannah and
Clint got there the parking lot was nearly ready to
overflow onto Center Street where it curved around
the town square. Clint managed to find what seemed
to be the last spot and backed into it. Then he turned
off the engine and reached behind the seat for a plaid
blanket.

Before Savannah realized what he was doing she
thought he was reaching for her. A rush of excitement
ran through her only to hit an abrupt dead end when
what he was really doing became clear.

As he got out and came around for her, she gave
herself a stern talking to. They were not a high school
couple like those around them who left cars and
walked arm in arm toward the rally. They were not a
couple at all. They were only two people who'd
known each other a long time ago and were now getting reacquainted, she told herself for what surely
must have been the hundredth time.

But whether that was true or not, she had difficulty
convincing herself. In the years they'd gone together
before Savannah had left Elk Creek, there had been
two full seasons of football games and rallies that

Savannah had sneaked out to attend with Clint as alumni. And as a couple.

And Savannah was having trouble fighting off some strong flashbacks.

She got out of the truck just as Clint was about to open the door for her, and jammed her hands into the pockets of the heavy pea coat she wore.

*Just old friends,* she told herself over and over again. *Just old acquaintances...*

But when he slipped his arm through the crook of hers she didn't feel mere friendship. His touch set off more of that warmth inside her and a sense of peace, of contentment, a sense that everything was right with the world. It also set off a whole lot of glittering sparks that tickled things into life that had no business being either alive or tickled or tingling with an eagerness for more. And she found it hard to distinguish which were flashbacks to a past that had no bearing on the present and what really *was* the present....

The football field was behind the school building. Savannah and Clint joined the crowd of people—young and not young—who were walking in that direction. The rally itself was actually being held farther out, past the field and the stands, in the open area beyond.

An enormous bonfire had been lit and folks had set out blankets all around it, giving it a wide berth. They'd also left an informal aisle from one end of the bleachers to the fire. The Elk Creek High football team would run out from the field, down the aisle, and line up in a circle around the bonfire as each of their names were called individually and the crowd welcomed them with cheers.

The Culhanes and the Hellers were all clustered together, waving and shouting for Savannah and Clint, who seemed to be the last to arrive. They joined everyone else, squeezing in and adding their blanket to the rest on the ground.

They sat cross-legged among so many family members and friends that the sense of being a couple was replaced by being just part of the group. Yet Savannah was still very, very aware of even small things about Clint. Like the feel of his knee brushing hers or his shoulder coming into contact with her shoulder.

And if fleeting fantasies—of his putting his arm around her, or moving to sit behind her rather than at her side and pulling her to rest against that hard chest—kept dancing through her mind, she worked diligently to ignore them and to tamp down any craving that went with them.

Spirits were high and revelry abounded as the school's cheerleaders preceded the football team into the limelight to rev up the crowd.

Amy, Randa and Linc's son, Danny, hopped and jumped and mimicked the girls' cheers as the adults added their voices where it was called for, and did plenty of hooting and hollering, clapping and woofing even when it wasn't.

No member of the team received less of an ovation than anyone else, and even in the light of only the fire it was obvious the boys were beaming.

It occurred to Savannah that there was a lot to be said for this small-town support, for a place where nearly the whole citizenry came out to pat its kids on the back. Sure, at her school in Cheyenne a fair share of the parents would attend something like this, but here even people who didn't have any stake in the events or the teenagers involved—like the Hellers and the Culhanes—still came out to cheer them on.

There was something special about that. And again she understood how Ivey had found herself feeling different about this place than they had as kids. How she could come back and make her life here again.

The rally went on until cheerleaders and folks alike were hoarse, and then the fireworks began.

The display rivaled the Fourth of July and brought enthusiasm to a climax before it ended. Then the school principal got on the loudspeaker again to wish the team good luck, invite the whole town to the game and the dance and thank everyone for coming out to show their support.

Steaming mugs of cider, hot dogs, chips, cookies and cakes were being served in the cafeteria and, with blankets tucked under arms, just about everyone filed into the school to get warm, mingle and have refreshments.

Savannah and Clint were no different, although rather than mingle separately, Clint never left Savannah's side—much to the dismay of a few single women who seemed to be in pursuit of him. They were forced to do their flirting with Savannah looking on.

And she didn't like it much.

She told herself in no uncertain terms that she had no claim on this man. That there was no reason the other women couldn't talk to him. Flirt with him. Flatter him. Fish for information about whether or not he was going to the homecoming dance and if he was, if he was going stag.

But she still didn't like it, and when Clint finally suggested they leave, she was only too happy to agree.

"I see the Culhanes are still woman magnets," she said on the way to his truck.

"Why, Savannah, that almost sounded jealous," he said as if it flattered him no end.

"I was only making an observation," she said, although she knew there had been a tinge of the green-eyed monster in her tone. "Seems strange, with how popular you Culhanes have always been, that not any of the three of you are married."

Clint opened the passenger-side door of his truck and waited while she got in.

Then he said, "Cully's engaged," and closed the door.

Savannah waited until he was behind the wheel and pulling out of the parking place to go on. "But what about you?"

"I'm not engaged."

And he was enjoying being stubborn about telling her what she wanted to know.

But Savannah was suddenly curious enough to be just as stubborn. "I can't believe you never married."

"What do you think? That I'm hidin' an ex-wife in the closet? You know better than that. Around here *nothin'* gets hidden for long. If I'd married you'd have heard about it. Probably all the way to Cheyenne."

That was true enough. Della would have told her. But Savannah's curiosity was still unappeased. "Seems I heard that you were pretty serious about someone a while back."

"I was. Thought I might end up married to her," he said easily enough as they headed out of town.

"But you didn't," she said to prod him to go on.

"We were talkin' about it. She was a feed sales-woman. Made her trips here longer and longer so we could see more of each other. Let me know she wouldn't be averse to stayin', puttin' down roots."

"But?" Savannah prompted again when he seemed to stall.

"But then I found out some things about her."

"She was really a man dressed as a woman, and one day you saw her on a TV talk show telling how she was pulling a big scam on you," Savannah guessed with the most outlandish scenario she could think of to spur him on.

Clint laughed. "Not quite. But she did get arrested."

"Arrested?" Della hadn't told her that, and she didn't know what was harder to believe—that her best friend had omitted a bit of gossip that juicy or that the sole woman Clint had gotten serious with in the past fifteen years had been arrested for something. "What for?" she asked with a voice full of her own astonishment.

"It seemed Franny—that was her name, Franny—had a son. About four years old. He'd been taken away from her because she'd let her last male friend beat on him. The court gave the boy to his father and ordered her to pay child support but she didn't do that, either, so there was a warrant out for her arrest, and when the sheriff got notice of it, he locked her up."

"Oh." Savannah hadn't expected that.

"It was pretty disillusionin'," Clint went on. "It shook me up to think I'd gotten that close to marryin' somebody who could let some damn idiot beat on her child and then keep a whole side of herself—of her past—a secret. Keep even the fact that she had a son a secret. If that's the sort of woman she was, the sort of mother—"

He stopped short.

Maybe because he'd glanced over at Savannah and could tell by the look on her face that she was making comparisons to herself, to having kept the secret of the baby from him, to letting her father wreak his havoc.

Or maybe because that was what he was thinking himself—that she wasn't altogether different from that other woman...

"Not a great story for tonight," he said in a hurry. "Anyway, truth to tell, I was worried about actually gettin' to the altar with her even before that. My feelin's for her seemed to be lackin' something."

He was attempting to put a better spin on this, and Savannah tried to go along. "What were your feelings lacking?"

He shrugged one of those broad shoulders. "Guess it was just that not-livin'-up-to-my-first-love thing you talked about before. So it was all for the best."

They'd reached the drive that led up to her house, by then. Clint turned onto it but stopped the truck just under the twenty-foot-tall wooden arch that dubbed this the Double H Ranch—or the Do ble H Ranch actually, since the *u* had gotten lost over the years and never been replaced.

Clint cut the engine and a confused Savannah said, "Is there something wrong with the truck?"

He smiled at her with that wicked smile he could flash when he wanted to and turned in her direction on the bench seat. This time when he stretched his arm across the back of it, it wasn't to pull a blanket from behind, the way he had earlier. He just let his arm rest there, his fingers toying with her hair where it brushed the top of the seat.

"You don't remember?" he asked with feigned injury at the very idea.

"Remember..." she repeated, trying to figure out what was going on.

"Our first date," he supplied. "I believe you told your father you were going to the library with a friend—without letting him know the friend wasn't a girl."

It didn't take more than that for Savannah to know what he had up his sleeve. "And when you took me home you couldn't drive all the way up to the house because then he might see you and know you weren't a girl. Besides, none of my girlfriends went right up to the house unless they absolutely had to. They dropped me off down here so they could avoid getting anywhere near my father, even in passing."

Clint's grin broadened to crease his cheeks; he was obviously pleased that she'd remembered.

"So do you want me to walk from here for old-time's sake?" she asked, joking.

He laughed. "Nope. That's not what I had in mind."

"Good, because it's snowing harder than it was earlier, and that's no short jaunt." Besides, if they were going to relive the ending of their first date she wanted to stick around for the whole thing....

"You were nervous as a rabbit with a fox sniffin' at its burrow," he reminisced.

"I'd lied to see you. And there I was, sitting in a truck with a *boy,* when I wasn't allowed to do anything as improper—according to my father—as date. Of course I was nervous."

"But in no hurry to go in just the same," he reminded her with a touch of ego tingeing his tone.

"I don't recall your being in any hurry to have me go in."

"True enough. Not before I got my good-night kiss. Your very first kiss, wasn't it?"

"You know it was." And for some reason she felt all over again that evening's anxiousness—and eagerness—to have Clint Culhane kiss her.

"I had to do a little teachin' that night."

"You weren't complaining."

"No, ma'am, I wasn't. In fact I got a big kick out of it."

"Lord, I hated being so inept at something so simple."

"You weren't inept. Just inexperienced."

He was easing closer to her as they talked. Much as he had that evening so long ago. As if approaching a wild mare that might bolt at any moment.

She wasn't retreating, but she wasn't moving forward, either. Instead she was just watching him come, suddenly thinking of the ways in which he'd changed since they'd last sat there like that. Of the fact that he was bigger, sturdier, stronger now than he had been at eighteen. That even though she'd thought then that he was a man, he hadn't been. He'd still been barely more than a boy. But there was no denying that he was a man now. Through and through. Full grown. Honed and handsome. And much, much too sexy for her own good....

"And there I was, with one of Elk Creek's notorious Culhane brothers," she heard herself say in a voice that had gone a little smoky, forcing herself to return to their reminiscing rather than stay too long in the more appealing—more dangerously tempting—here and now.

"Notorious?" he said as if he'd been wrongly accused.

"Yes, notorious. You and your brothers and my cousins. You guys got around."

"We were all just lookin' for the right girl," he said as if he were pure as the snow falling all around them. "But I knew that night, sittin' here under the sign, that I'd found her."

"You lie like a dog," she joked again.

"No, ma'am," he repeated. "Not that I knew what it meant to have found the right girl. Or what it would mean later on. I just knew that I'd never been with any other girl who'd made me not care if I was ever with anyone else again."

"Ah, so when you were with other girls you were just thinking about the next conquest?"

His grin turned sheepish. "Don't make it sound so bad."

He was smoothing the back of her head with his right hand in slow, soothing strokes. The scent of his aftershave lingered only faintly, but it was enough to go to her head. And even in the dimness of the truck cab, where the only light came from the gray-white sky beyond it, she could see how terrific looking he was with his chiseled, masculine features; that hair that partly stood up, partly waved back; and those eyes…those penetrating, mesmerizing eyes.…

"As I recall," he said in a quiet, husky voice as if someone might overhear. "I had to take your chin in my hand, like so.…" He did that with his left hand, tucking his thumb just under the tip of her chin and riding her jawline with the side of his index finger. "I had to tilt your head up because you kept looking down at your lap, as if you were afraid to look at me."

He applied only the gentlest of pressure to raise her chin so her face was at the perfect angle to his. "And I barely kissed you that first time," he said just before he touched his mouth to hers in a brief, scant, eminently patient buss as tender as that one so long ago.

Then he drew back only an inch or two and chuckled. "And you blushed to high heaven," he said, as if it still delighted him.

Those same glittering sparks he'd set off inside her earlier with only the linking of his arm through hers came alive again, tickling, tingling, leaving her just as eager for more.

"It didn't take long before I was an old hand, though," she remarked, knowing she was urging him on, that she probably shouldn't be, but was unable to resist nonetheless.

"But that night I had to take your arms and put them around me," he continued, doing that now, draping them over his shoulders where she clasped them behind his neck. "And I had to tell you it was okay to relax your lips a little. Even open them some..."

Savannah laughed at that. "And to close my eyes. You had to tell me to close my eyes."

"Close your eyes, sweet Savannah," he commanded.

She did, not caring if this was a game that could get her into trouble. Wanting only to do exactly what she was doing.

Clint touched her mouth with his again, only this time it stayed. His lips parted, and that was all it took to ignite the sort of passion that had swept her off her feet so long ago, that had wiped away all thought, all common sense, all inhibitions.

His tongue coaxed her lips to part farther and then came to invite hers to play—not something he'd done that first time, but it seemed perfectly natural now.

His arms closed around her, pulled her to the hard wall of his chest and held her there as one hand cradled her head so he could deepen the kiss even more.

A new craving surged through Savannah, and she unclasped her own hands from behind his neck to lay her palms on his back. To fill them with the feel of his muscles beneath coat and turtleneck, powerful enough to stretch both fabrics and still roll beneath the massage she was unwittingly giving.

The past and the present mingled then, and nothing mattered but that Clint was holding her. That her breasts were nestled into his chest. That he was kissing her, caressing her in a way that lit flames in her blood, that made her nerve endings fly to the surface of her skin, that made her senses reel and her whole body turn pliable, achingly willing for the touch of hands she remembered all too well.

And then lights suddenly flooded the truck cab.

For a moment Savannah thought the brightness was coming from inside her. That it was some brilliant burst that went along with the pleasure of that kiss and all it was arousing in her.

Then a horn honked and she realized that someone had pulled into the drive behind them.

"Dammit!" Clint muttered as he and Savannah parted.

With an arm still around her they both looked out the rear window into the beams of headlights.

"Cully," Clint said, sounding aggravated.

Then his brother rolled down his window, stuck his head out and called, "Bathroom!"

"Amy or Randa," Clint said by way of explanation, more resigned now.

"And they can't wait, and we're blocking the way," Savannah finished.

Clint slid back behind the wheel, started the engine again and spewed gravel getting up the drive as quickly as he could, with Cully fast on his tail.

When they got there Ivey jumped out of the other truck, followed close behind by Amy and Cully, who was carrying Randa and making a dash for the porch.

The whole thing was comical to watch, and Savannah couldn't help laughing, which dissolved what little remained of the romantic moment she and Clint had been sharing.

"I'd better go in," she said then, while she still had some wits about her, which meant before anything got started up again.

"You don't *have* to," Clint answered as if he were a sinner tempting a saint, making her smile at his deviltry.

"I think it's best."

He nodded in the direction of the house. "You need a fast dash to the bathroom, too?"

"No, I just think it's time to call it a night before we do any more strolling down memory lane."

"We never left the truck."

"That's the problem."

"Didn't feel like a problem to me."

That streak of incorrigibleness was showing again. But as charming as he was, as tempted as she was to indulge herself a while longer, she worked to ignore both the charm and the temptation. "Good night, Clint," she said with one hand on the door handle.

"We're still on for the game tomorrow night, aren't we?" he said then, conceding.

"I was planning on it."

"Okay, then. I guess I can let you go now."

"Oh, good. I hate it when my dates hold me hostage," she joked.

"Does it get 'em what they want?"

"Almost never. But I guess that depends on what it is they want."

"You. I want you."

She couldn't tell if he was still kidding around or if he was serious. He sounded pretty serious. And there seemed to be an intensity in his eyes that hadn't been there before.

But if he meant what he said, she didn't know how to respond to it, so she pretended he was kidding and said, "Yeah, sure, that's what they all say." She opened the door then, and as he began to do the same from his side, she said, "No, don't get out. You don't have to walk me up."

"Are you tellin' me that even if I do I won't be gettin' a good-night kiss?"

"Didn't you already get one of those?"

"A person can always tolerate more than one."

"Not with an audience, though."

He sighed elaborately. "So this is my reward for lettin' those two little stinkers have that last cup of cider?"

Savannah smiled at his mock lament and hopped out of the truck. "Good night."

He grumbled.

"Remember, they're only little girls with tiny bladders, so be a good sport."

"Good sport. Good night. Nothin' good that I can see about this."

She gave in to a sudden urge to step up on the running board, lean into the cab and kiss him one quick peck on the lips.

"Okay, so that's pretty good. Could be better—it *was* better a few minutes ago—but pretty good just the same."

"See you tomorrow night," she said as she backed out of the truck again and closed the door.

But even though she'd teased him about the interruption of what had been going on between them, she couldn't say that she was glad it had happened, either.

She knew she should have been, because that kiss could well have gone much further than it had with the way she'd lost herself to it, to being in his arms.

But even so, she wasn't glad it had been cut short. She couldn't be.

Not when, like it or not, wise or not, the evening hadn't been only a stroll down memory lane.

It had been more than that.

A lot more.

So much more that she found it easy to understand why she'd fallen in love with him all those years ago.

And hard to accept that the kiss—and everything else between her and Clint—couldn't just go on and on...

Forever.

## Chapter Seven

Clint was pouring himself a cup of coffee just after dawn the next morning when Cully came into the kitchen.

"Mornin'," Clint mumbled with a scant glance up to see who had joined him. He'd been awake for half an hour, had showered, shaved and dressed, but he was still loggy after a night spent lying in bed doing more thinking than sleeping.

"Okay, go ahead," Cully said resignedly. "Slug me if you want to for interruptin' you last night." He held open his arms to expose his shirt-clad belly as the target he was offering.

Clint took a slower, sleepy-eyed look over his shoulder. "Don't tempt me," he said, knowing full well Cully was referring to the kiss he'd had to cut short the previous evening to make Clint move his truck out of Savannah's drive.

But rather than punch Cully, Clint handed him the coffee mug and poured another for himself.

"Funny place to stop for a good-night kiss," Cully observed once he'd accepted the bracing black beverage that the brothers brewed to get their day started.

Clint sweetened his coffee but didn't offer any explanations.

"Looked like a choice smooch, though," his brother went on, anyway. "I'd have rated it For Mature Audiences Only."

Clint took a drink from the mug he held like a glass and turned to face his brother, leaning his hips against the counter's edge. Still he didn't say anything. He only smiled slightly at the memory of just how choice that kiss had been.

"Things happenin' between the two of you?" Cully persisted.

"Things like kissin' her good-night," was all Clint would say.

"And you don't want to talk about anything else that might be goin' on."

"Nothin' *to* talk about. We're gettin' to know each other again, is all."

"Gettin' to know each other pretty well from what I saw."

Clint just smiled once more. He knew his brother was partly goading him, partly fishing for information. But he wasn't going to fall for the goading, and there wasn't any information to give.

Clint himself didn't know exactly what was going on between him and Savannah. And since he still hadn't told either of his brothers about the baby they'd lost fifteen years ago and what had come of that, there wasn't much he could say that wouldn't require telling the whole story he didn't want to tell. Not yet, at any rate. Not before he could figure out what it all meant in terms of the present and how he felt about it.

"You know, we're all pretty sure you never stopped carin' about Savannah," Cully said then, a bit more serious than he'd been before. "Which makes me think it won't take much for you to be in over your head again. What happens if this second round doesn't work out?"

"I guess it doesn't work out."

"Be like another mule kick."

Clint agreed with a raising of his chin.

"I hope you're bein' careful."

"Is this a condom talk?" Clint joked. "Because if it is, *Dad,* we haven't gotten to know each other all *that* well so you can relax."

"It's not a condom talk. I'm just sayin' for you to keep in mind that Savannah hasn't cut any ties with that life of hers up in Cheyenne."

"Neither had Ivey until you persuaded her to."

"You doin' some persuadin'?"

Clint chuckled wryly. "I don't know what I'm doin'," he said honestly.

"But you'll take care of yourself," Cully reiterated. "I wouldn't want to see you the way you were when Savannah left before. I thought you were gonna drink and fight yourself into an early grave."

"Crazy times," Clint conceded.

"Don't let 'em come again."

With his message apparently delivered, Cully took his coffee and left Clint alone in the kitchen again.

*Crazy times...*

Clint's own words echoed in his mind.

Crazy and confusing.

And he wasn't sure the present was too much saner or more clear to him than that period fifteen years ago had been.

He was just as confused, that was for sure.

Talking about Franny and the one relationship that had gotten him close to marriage to anyone other than Savannah definitely added to the confusion factor. As if what he felt for Savannah and the whole past-present thing wasn't enough.

It had seemed to him as he'd told Savannah about his former fiancée that he'd hit too close to home in some way.

And that bothered him.

Maybe Savannah had just been horrified by what Franny had allowed to happen to her child. But Clint didn't think so. Savannah had actually turned red in the face, as if he were talking about her, about something she'd done and was embarrassed—mortified—by. As if he were talking about their lost child.

It left him wondering why.

As far as he could tell, the similarities between Franny letting some guy beat on her son, losing custody and then not even supporting the boy, and Savannah taking a slap and a shove from her father that had caused a miscarriage weren't all that profound. So why had telling her about Franny had the effect it had on her?

Was there something about Savannah that he

wasn't seeing? Something that made her compare herself with Franny and come up with a likeness?

There was no denying that they *had* both kept secrets from him. Big secrets. And maybe that was what had struck a nerve with Savannah.

But he couldn't help worrying that there was more to it than that.

And the truth was, Cully's warning to be cautious had come on top of Clint giving himself that same advice after hours of thinking about it all through the night.

He needed to be careful.

Not so much because he thought Savannah was the kind of person Franny had proved to be. But because for some reason, Savannah thought she was. And maybe it would be a good idea to know why.

One difference had stood out in his mind as he'd talked about Franny, though. One very big difference between what was going on with Savannah and what had gone on with Franny. And that difference was in his own reaction to learning the secrets each of them had kept from him.

Finding out about Franny had made his feelings for her stop cold.

But that hadn't happened with Savannah.

In fact, the revelation of her secret hadn't even slowed the progression of feelings that were snowballing—building in power, in intensity, in momentum, with each minute he spent with her.

It hadn't altered his enjoyment of her. His pleasure in the simple sight of her smile.

It certainly hadn't made him want her any less.

And, man, did he want her! With every nerve ending, with every inch of his body, with every breath he took, he wanted her....

But he intended to be careful just the same. Because in spite of all he finally understood about what had happened fifteen years ago, he had a strong sense that there was just as much that he didn't understand about what was going on with Savannah now.

At least he intended to be as careful as he could be.

But careful or not, the odds that he was in line for another mule kick to the gut seemed pretty high, anyway.

Because when he thought about her leaving to go back to her life in Cheyenne, he realized that it would be as hard on him right at that minute as it had been all those years ago. He was already in that deep with her.

So he'd be careful, but it probably wouldn't really help much. Except maybe to give him fair warning when that next mule kick might be coming.

And in the meanwhile, he had this time with her now.

And that was something.

That was surely something....

He just hoped it was enough to cushion the blow if that kick came down the road.

Savannah spent the afternoon in Elk Creek with Ivey, shopping for homecoming dresses and enjoying the frivolity of something they'd neither one done as teenagers.

Along the way Savannah also bought a new pair of jeans—a tad tighter than she usually wore—and a warm, fleecy white top that buttoned from the waist-skimming hem to the rib-knit turtleneck collar.

Ivey didn't say anything about the kiss she and Cully had driven in on the night before, which Savannah was grateful for, and so the two sisters had a leisurely several hours going in and out of the small town's stores, reacquainting themselves with what Elk Creek had to offer and generally having a nice day.

When they headed home they picked up burgers and fries at the Dairy King for dinner, and by the time Clint and Cully pulled up in front of the house in their separate trucks that evening, both Savannah and Ivey were showered, combed, made-up, dressed and ready to go.

They didn't wait for either man to come to the door, but grabbed warm coats and went out to climb into the truck cabs themselves.

"Well, hi, there," Clint said, sounding slightly surprised as Savannah put a little bounce in her entrance into his truck.

"Hi, there, to you, too," she countered, feeling as young—and as carefree—as if she were a student going to the big homecoming football game rather than an alumnus.

Clint's face eased into an amused smile. "You must have had a great day. You look like you're sittin' on top of the world."

"I thought I was," she teased him about the high-rise vehicle, making a show of looking down as if from a lofty perch.

"Don't go makin' fun of this ol' girl. She's been good to me," he pretended to reprimand, rubbing the dashboard lovingly.

Savannah tried not to wish that big hand was caressing her instead, but it was no easy task. "You look pretty fine yourself," she said before she'd thought about it.

Not that it wasn't true. It was. He had on black jeans and a matching jacket over a silver-gray shirt that was open halfway down his chest to expose a black turtleneck T-shirt. All this somehow accentuated the lines and planes of his oh-so-handsome face, making it look lean, angular, masculine and a little like an Old West desperado. But still, telling him how delicious he looked seemed more flirty than she ordinarily was.

Apparently it pleased him to hear it, though, because his smile broadened into a grin. "You really are perky tonight."

"Perky?" she repeated with a groan. "I'm just looking forward to the game, being out in the autumn air—"

"Snugglin' up on the bleachers to keep warm...."

She gave him a we'll-see smile.

"Or you could scoot on over here close to me now, and we could get a head start on it," he suggested with a wicked wiggle to his eyebrows.

"Too much temptation for you not to keep your hands on the wheel," she countered, even as her whole body cried out for her to do just as he'd said and slide across the bench seat to sit next to him. To have her shoulder against his much bigger, broader, harder one. Her leg along the length of his bolelike thigh. Basking in the scent of that heady aftershave he had on again...

But she didn't do it.

Thwarted but undaunted, he said, "I'm gonna get you over here eventually, wait and see."

"I can't tell—is that a threat or a promise?" Where was this stuff coming from? This was not like her. On the other hand, it felt kind of good to step out of character for a change.

Clint laughed. "Threat, promise—it's whatever you want it to be, sweetheart."

Then he put the truck back in gear and pulled away from the house to follow the trail Cully had left down the drive.

"Does your school in Cheyenne have a football team?" Clint asked as he did.

"We used to. Up until about three years ago we were considered a junior high—grades seven, eight and nine—and the ninth-graders had a team. But then the county I'm in changed things because of enrollment rises. Now we're a middle school—grades six, seven and eight. Ninth-graders are freshmen at the high school, and we don't have a football team anymore. Except in gym class. They play a little there."

"How'd you decide to be a teacher, anyway? You never talked about doin' that before you left."

"I just started leaning toward it in college. I can't really say why. Maybe because school was always a refuge for me as a kid, so I was drawn back to that to work."

"Is it still a refuge?"

For some reason that sounded as if she were hiding out in her job. Or maybe that was just how it struck Savannah, because the longer she was in Elk Creek, spending time with Clint, enjoying herself, the more she was coming to see that submerging herself in her work, being a workaholic, really was a way to avoid having much of a personal life in Cheyenne.

"I guess it is still sort of a refuge," she admitted, wondering why she had the sense that her work would somehow be less fulfilling when she got back to it after this.

But they were at the school by then, and talk turned to trying to locate a vacant parking place.

Tonight the lot was full, so Clint found a spot on the street, and they walked in with a whole herd of other folks. Once they were at the field they again joined the rest of the Hellers and the Culhanes in the stands.

Snow wasn't falling but the temperature was still low enough for each breath to leave a cloud in the air. It was prime football weather and a good excuse for couples to huddle together for warmth.

As Clint and Savannah situated themselves on the bleachers, Clint stretched an arm around her and pulled her as close to him as he possibly could.

"Gotcha!" he said, as if he'd gotten his way here if not earlier in the truck when he'd joked about getting her to snuggle up next to him on that seat.

But Savannah didn't complain. Or move away. It felt too good to be there, and she didn't have a single thought of putting any distance whatsoever between them.

Unfortunately his arm didn't stay around her throughout the whole game. It just wasn't feasible no matter how much she would have liked it. And she would have liked it a lot.

Clint did put it back now and then, leaning near to ask if she was too cold or needed something, or when enthusiasm for a particularly exciting play carried him away, or for no reason except that he seemed to want to.

And each time it set off a rush of pleasure through her that made her begin to wait for those moments the way a child waits for a glimpse of Santa Claus.

The game ended in a win for Elk Creek, and Jackson invited all the Culhanes and Hellers home for hot, buttered rum to warm up.

Talk between town and Jackson's house, and long after they'd arrived at Jackson's house and were drinking the liquid warmth, centered on the football game and football games of days gone by when all the men had played.

Savannah wasn't a huge fan of the sport, but it didn't matter because as everyone gathered around her cousin's fireplace, mostly sitting on the floor with their steaming mugs, Clint positioned himself behind her, the way she'd imagined him the night before. His long legs straddled her hips, he braced her back against his chest, wrapped his free arm around her shoulders to hold her there, and for all the world he made it seem as if those fifteen years had never separated them. As if they'd spent every moment of them just the way they were there on Jackson's floor—together.

Savannah had only one complaint with the evening, as it drew to a close and good-nights were being said. And that was that however close she and Clint had been, they still hadn't been alone for most of it.

As they headed out to his truck, Clint held her hand and led her to the driver's side to get in. It occurred to her then that all he had to do was take her across the road and that would be the end of her time with him. And she was not nearly ready for that.

"Is the lake still there or has it dried up?" she heard herself ask as he tossed the stadium jackets neither of them had put on again into the truck's cab and then handed her up after them.

"It's still there," Clint confirmed.

Throwing the coats across to the passenger's side had left Savannah only so much seat to slide onto. Plus Clint's helping hand up also kept her from sliding to the opposite end and so he managed to keep her where he apparently intended for her to be—next to him.

"Want to see it?" he asked when he was settled behind the wheel, putting a hint of wickedness into his tone.

Savannah had had just enough hot buttered rum to make her relax and to have a pretty loose grip on the inhibitions that usually guided her. So, without compunction, she said, "Sure. It's not all *that* late yet."

Clint smiled at her, a smile that imparted just how pleased he was. "Yes, ma'am. Whatever you say."

He hit the gas with a sudden jab that spewed gravel from behind the rear tires and announced that he was only too willing to go to the spot where they'd spent many an hour parked in a truck not as nice as the one he had now. Talking. And kissing. And more than kissing....

It was a small lake in a secluded area that bordered the Culhane property and the property Savannah and Ivey had inherited from their father. Property the Culhanes had offered to buy from Savannah and Ivey before Ivey and Cully had become engaged. Now marriage would join the two families and ranches alike.

Giant fir trees surrounded all but a third of the lake, and Clint came to a stop in that clear third, several feet back from the water's edge.

He turned off the engine, and silence fell around them. A peaceful silence that enveloped them, that lulled Savannah into even more relaxation.

Clint straightened out his arm along the seat back, dropping a hand to her shoulder to trail featherlight strokes there that might have been almost imperceptible through the heavy fleece of her shirt except that every nerve in her body was standing up to take notice of even the slightest contact between them.

"This is nice," she breathed, letting her head fall to his arm so she could glance up at him.

The moon was full and reflected off the not-yet-frozen lake to ricochet a creamy glow into the truck. It barely washed Clint's features, but it was enough for her to feast on what an incredibly striking man he'd become.

"Nice as anything I can imagine," he agreed. "I think I could spend the rest of my life sitting here like this."

Savannah looked straight ahead, out the windshield at the lake, then, because looking at him was too heady. It stirred up too many things in her that shouldn't be stirred up.

Besides, he was staring out at the water, too, and positioned like that it seemed as if they were two kids lying on a freshly mown summer's lawn, watching clouds, letting their minds wander wherever they might, daydreaming out loud.

And in that spirit, she said, "But since you can't spend the rest of your life sitting here like this, how do you intend to spend it?"

Clint shrugged a work-hardened shoulder and when he put it down again he let his hand drift to the side of her neck, caressing it absentmindedly in those same feathery strokes with the backs of his fingers.

"Pretty much the way I've spent my life up till now, I suppose," he answered. "Here, on the ranch. Working with my brothers."

"That's it?" she teased him, as if working the ranch with his brothers wasn't enough. "You're just going to be some old bachelor cowpoke?"

He chuckled wryly at that description. "No, that's not *it*. I'd like to get married," he added. "I'd like to have a big family—four or five kids. Six, maybe—to keep the numbers even."

"Same as always," she said because it was what they'd talked about as teenagers. Only then, when he'd talked about getting married he had meant to her, and now, he didn't say it with any particular aim. It was just marriage in general. To anyone. To someone other than her. And that fact suddenly rubbed her the wrong way.

"What about you?" he asked into her struggle to combat the unreasonable irritation running through her. "How do you mean to spend the rest of your life?"

It took her a moment to get back to the peaceful feelings, but she finally managed, and that was when she answered him. "Oh, I want to finish my thesis so I can go back to teaching."

"Feelin' the need for refuge, are you?" he teased gently with a tinge of innuendo in his deep voice.

"No, I just miss teaching," was all she'd admit to, even though her life back home did seem like a haven from feelings such as those she'd just had at the thought of Clint married to someone else.

"What about outside of work? Or are you just gonna be an old spinster schoolmarm?"

Savannah grimaced at that, not liking it any better than he'd liked the sound of *old bachelor cowpoke.* "Ick!"

"Well?" he challenged with a laugh at her response.

"I don't know," she hedged, because suddenly she had the niggling suspicion that what she'd like in her personal life was not very different from what she'd wanted as a teenager, either—to be Clint Culhane's wife, mother to those six kids of his....

But that ace had been discarded from her hand a long time ago, and she told herself it wasn't even something she should be thinking about. "I just don't know," she repeated.

"Let's see if we can narrow it down," he suggested, sounding very much like a participant in summer lawn woolgathering, as if none of this had any more validity than that. "Is the call of the big city still in your blood, or has bein' back in Elk Creek rung any bells?"

Savannah played along in the same vein. "It hasn't been *all* bad being here," she joked. Then she added, "I guess if I try really hard I can see why Ivey is willing to come back."

"Are you absolutely, totally and completely

against ever getting married or is it just an if-the-right-guy-comes-along kind of thing?''

''Hmm...I guess it's the right-guy kind of thing. Or maybe I'll just be a world traveler. The wacky, bohemian maiden aunt to Ivey and Cully's children. The one who drops in from parts unknown to shower them with shrunken heads and real China dolls and orchids from the rain forest.''

''Ivey and Cully,'' he repeated as if putting the two of them together was still difficult to grasp. And that was all it took to change the direction of their musings. ''Who would have ever thought it would be Cully and Ivey gettin' together and not you and me?''

''It is pretty strange,'' she agreed. ''I guess that means we'll be brother-in-law and sister-in-law instead of...anything else.''

This time it was Clint who grimaced. ''Brother and sister? Us?'' he said, sounding so horrified it made Savannah smile up at him again.

''It might not be so bad,'' she teased, giving in to an urge to raise one finger into the dimpled crease of his cheek and following it to his sharp jawbone.

He looked down at her with wicked delight in his expression. ''Sweetheart, it isn't your brother I *ever* wanted to be.''

''Brother-*in-law*.''

''Still.''

He was looking into her eyes. He raised the hand at her neck to brush her cheek with the backs of his fingers again in a tender caress, and all of a sudden the air around them seemed to change.

Staring up into his chiseled features, feeling his body close beside her, having his arm around her, his hand on her face, made Savannah's heart swell so much with feelings for him that it was as if she could actually feel it beating.

"Sorry," he said with a small smile that deepened only one dimple as his crystal blue eyes delved into hers. "But I don't see a wacky bohemian in there. And I sure as hell don't see a *sister*—in-law or not."

"Yeah?" She'd intended to make that sound like a joke but there was a huskiness to her voice that betrayed what had sprung to life inside her. "What do you see?"

"Savannah. My sweet, sweet Savannah..."

His thumb found its way beneath her chin, tipping her face a tad higher as his mouth came down to meet hers, and again time slipped away and they could have been teenagers who'd discovered each other belatedly, fallen in love and found the spot by the lake to indulge in the joy of being alone together.

Clint's lips parted and so did Savannah's. His tongue came to say hello and she met it with her own, letting the kiss deepen naturally.

Somehow they'd both turned on the seat to face each other. Clint closed his arms around her, cradling her head, holding her as tenderly as if she were something very delicate and he needed to contain the power in his arms so he didn't crush her.

Savannah slid her arms under his, laying her hands against his broad back, learning all over again the hills and valleys of that work-honed expanse that hadn't been anywhere near as solid, as developed, as sexy, when he was a bare blush of a man.

And then they weren't only sitting through kisses that grew more and more heated, more and more passionate. Savannah was lying back on the pile their coats made and Clint was over her, his weight partially on her in a way that felt wonderfully heavy.

She ignored the little voice in the back of her mind that warned her to take it easy. To take it slow. Not to get carried away. And instead she couldn't resist pulling his shirttails free of his jeans to slip her hands under the two layers of clothing he wore and slide them up the length of his back, to feel the smooth warmth of his skin, to revel in even that small amount of more-intimate contact she was craving.

Clint must have taken it as a signal.

To be honest, that was probably what she'd been giving him, because when his hands traveled a similar path under the back of her shirt she could only moan with pleasure at that first touch of his kid-leather palms to her bare skin.

Their kisses were openmouthed and eager, frenzied with desire by then, and that little voice of caution in Savannah's mind was all but silenced as her senses took over, as she breathed in the scent of Clint's aftershave. As she tasted the hot buttered rum on his breath. As every nerve in her body tuned in to his where it pressed against her; where soft curves met hard masculine ridges; where his hands massaged her back much as she wished they would massage her front....

As if he knew the longing that was going through her, one of those gifted hands finally slid around to her side. To her flat stomach. And upward...

She cursed whoever had invented bras, when Clint closed that hand over her breast, and the lacy cup kept her from feeling it fully. Cursed herself for wearing the thing and wished she could will it to disappear from between them.

Until Clint made a game of sneaking inside, letting his fingers curve into it to caress the mound of her breast with the backs of his fingers the way he'd caressed her cheek with them before, reaching far enough so that his buffed nails just grazed her nipple, teasing it into a yearning, straining kernel.

Then, with the hand that still braced her back, he unsnapped her bra and slipped completely underneath it at last. Closing a warm, adept palm over her breast, letting her nipple kiss the deepest curve of it as if it had found home.

No touch had been—could ever be—as wonderful as that first feel of his warm, strong hand cupping her breast at last. Covering it, kneading it, exploring it, circling the crest, rolling it between gentle fingers, pinching, tugging, driving her so wild her head fell away from his kiss.

Clint pressed his lips to her arched neck, flicking his tongue into the hollow and leaving tiny wet spots to air-dry and arouse the surface of her skin even more as he went on working such wonders at her breast.

Oh, clothes…there were too many clothes, Savannah thought in mindless passion that demanded to be sated. That cried out to shed every last piece of cloth that kept them apart. That put any barrier between his long, hard, masculine body and her softer one. Between her striving flesh and what it was striving for. She wanted to be naked in his arms. She wanted him to be naked in hers. She wanted there to be no inch of him that was kept from her touch. Right then. Right there....

Except that suddenly that little voice in her head found more volume, reminding her that she wasn't a teenager anymore. That these weren't the old days. That the bond between her and Clint was not as definite, not as defined as the bond that had been between them years ago.

And that maybe letting passion have its way was not what she should be doing with this man who wanted things in his life that she might not be the right person to give....

"No. No more," she said. Groaned, actually, as if she were in pain. Which she was, although not in any physical sense.

It seemed to take a moment for her words to penetrate Clint's consciousness, but when they did, he stopped cold. He moved his hand down to her side once more and raised his head from the path it was taking between shirt buttons that had somehow come undone.

He took a deep breath and blew it out as if that would give him some control, dropping his forehead to her collarbone.

"Wow," he said quietly, more to himself than to her, his breath a hot gust against her awakened skin, sounding as if he, too, had been lost in passion so powerful it had surpassed all reason.

Then he said, "I guess we've still got it, huh?"

She knew what he meant. He meant they still had the chemistry between them that could light fire in the blood and leave them both pawns to the desire it set aflame.

Clint sat up and took Savannah with him, running his hands through his hair as she resituated her bra and hooked it.

Then he looked into her eyes once more and reached a tender palm to her cheek. "I want you, Savannah," he confessed. "But not if you don't want…to."

It wasn't that she didn't want to do exactly what they were doing. And lots more. It wasn't that she didn't want him. She did. Too much.

But she just wasn't sure she should indulge in it. Not when it wasn't clear where either of them were headed. Where this new relationship was headed. If it was headed anywhere at all.

"It just isn't the right time…the right place," she said quietly to alleviate any thought he might have about her feelings for him.

Clint nodded as if he understood and agreed.

Then he started the truck again and drove the short distance to her house without either of them saying anything else.

But when he'd pulled up in front of the porch, Savannah couldn't just get out and leave things hanging.

"I suppose I could say that I shouldn't have suggested we go out to the lake."

"You could say it. But I'm not sorry you did suggest it. Or that we went."

"Neither am I." She almost whispered her admission.

Clint reached a hand to her cheek again, stroking it with fingertips that seemed too sexy to be soothing. Certainly they aroused things again inside her that were anything but calm.

Then he said, "But you're right. If we take this any further it can't be in this truck, like two carried-away kids."

She was tempted to ask him where they would do it, but refrained. It was only playing with more of that fire that could all too easily be relit.

"Are we still on for the dance tomorrow night?" he asked then.

"I'm looking forward to it." And to wearing the new dress she'd bought. And most of all, to just being with him again.

"Me, too," he said simply, smiling a smile that was like balm to a sore muscle.

Then he opened the door and got out, helping her to follow suit and keeping hold of her hand once she had. He led her up onto the porch where he kissed her again. A short good-night kiss laced around the edges with that unsatisfied, smoldering passion that was still just below the surface.

"'Night," he said after ending the kiss and sighing out a breath that let her know it wasn't easy for him to leave.

But leave he did. Before she'd even gone inside. As if he had to go right then or he wouldn't be able to go at all.

And as Savannah finally went inside after she'd watched him drive off, she couldn't help but wonder if where they were headed was anyplace but into each other's arms.

Because she couldn't seem to think beyond that.

Not when it was what she wanted more than she'd wanted anything in a long, long time.

Maybe, heaven help her, more than she'd wanted anything in the whole of the last fifteen years....

## Chapter Eight

Ivey's wedding shower was the next afternoon at her cousin Kansas's house. By one o'clock the small frame home was filled to the brim with Elk Creek women—young, old and in-between.

Jackson's wife, Ally, catered a buffet luncheon with a sangria punch that made everyone slightly giddy, and after they played a few games, Ivey got down to the business of opening gifts.

Kansas announced that she had orders to put in a telephone call to Della just before Ivey opened the present Della had sent, so when the brightly wrapped package came up Kansas did just that.

After hellos to everyone through the speakerphone, Della explained her present—a beautifully ornate Victorian doorknob. With a lock. It was intended for the newlyweds' bedroom door since Ivey was marrying into a ready-made family complete with kids who—like most kids—would rarely remember to knock before barging in.

Everyone laughed and added their own comments, and then, after Della said a general goodbye, Savannah finished the call privately on the extension in the kitchen while Ivey went on with the shower.

Concerned about her friend, Savannah wanted to know how Della really was underneath the forced gaiety she'd shown to the party.

Della assured her she and the kids were okay, that they had good days and bad days, but that it helped to be with her folks.

Then they said goodbye, too, and Savannah returned to the living room.

"Well, what do you say, Savannah?" Mona Dray, the butcher's wife, asked as Savannah sat on the floor near Ivey's chair.

"What do *I* say or do you mean what did Della say just now on the phone?" Savannah asked for clarification because she'd obviously come in in the middle of something, and she didn't have the foggiest idea what the elderly butcher's wife was asking.

"What do *you* say. We were talking about you and Clint Culhane and wondering if the next wedding shower we go to will be yours."

"I don't think so," Savannah answered in a hurry, laughing as if the other woman was kidding, even though the tone was more one of challenge than of teasing.

"So the two of you are just recapturing your youth?" Mona persisted.

Before Savannah had a chance to say anything to

that, Nancy Dray—Mona's thirty-five-year-old grand-daughter—piped up. "Clint and Savannah. Savannah and Clint. Savannah came back to town, and the two of them fell in together just out of old habit. You know how hard old habits are to break. But that's all there is to it."

As if Savannah had said that herself, Mona aimed her response at her, "Then don't take too long, because we know a few ladies who have their caps set for those single Culhanes. If you're just revisiting the glory days, then get it done with so someone else can have the here and now."

Kansas, who was sitting near Savannah, pretended to cough, and behind her hand whispered, "And Nancy Dray is one of those ladies who has her cap set for Clint, in case you haven't guessed."

Then Kansas urged Ivey to go on opening presents, successfully changing the subject.

But for Savannah the subject wasn't so easily left behind. The other women's phrases repeated themselves in her mind.

*Recapturing youth. Revisiting the glory days. Old habits...*

The terms all made it sound as if what was happening between her and Clint didn't have much to do with that "here and now" the butcher's wife had referred to. As if there was nothing of any substance to it. And Savannah couldn't help wondering about that herself.

Were she and Clint just on replay?

Maybe in some ways.

She had to admit to herself that their times together hadn't had the same tone that a date with just any man in Cheyenne would have had. Things like the homecoming game the previous night, like going to the dance tonight, made her feel more like a teenager—at least, like the carefree teenager she *should* have been all those years ago—than a grown woman.

But what if she factored out what they'd actually done and thought only about what it was like to be with him? What if Clint was just a man she had had a few dates with? What if she took away the element of having known him before? Of their having a past? Would the same things be happening between them? Would the same feelings be awakening?

In her mind she blocked out the image of the Clint Culhane of fifteen years ago and only let herself focus on the person he was today, trying to judge from that standpoint with a more objective eye.

No one could dispute the fact that he was dropdead gorgeous. That she would have been initially attracted to him on that score. She and any number of women whose heads turned when he walked into a room.

It didn't require an objective eye to see the current appeal of a six-foot-three-inch mountain of hard muscle and sinew; of a face no plastic surgeon could improve upon; of hair that made her want to run her fingers through it the way he often did; of a voice as deep and rich as Belgian dark chocolate.

But what about after the initial attraction that might have gotten him a first date? Would there have been a second, third or fourth date if they weren't tiptoeing through the tulips of time? If they weren't playing around with old emotions that might not have any validity now?

It didn't take her long to know that there would have been more than one date.

The Clint of today made their time together pleasant and lighthearted. He was unfailingly kind. And sweet. And attentive. He was just an all-round nice guy who was also sensitive, polite, inventive, imaginative and charming. Plus there was no disputing that he was intelligent. Dropped Gs from his words or not, there were brains behind that drawl, or he and his brothers would never have been able to build their ranch the way they had. He was calm and patient, even-tempered—so even-tempered that he'd kept cool when he'd had the right to blow up at her after she'd told him about the long-ago miscarriage. There was nothing vindictive about him. Or arrogant. He didn't have a chip on his shoulder—just one of many things she'd discovered in other men along the way.

And Savannah was beginning to feel like his press agent with so many accolades running through her mind.

Not that any of it wasn't true. It was. There was no denying that Clint Culhane was all that on top of being a down-to-earth guy with a sexy smile, a sexy swagger, a sexy everything to boot.

And Savannah finally came to the conclusion that whether she'd known him ten lifetimes or ten days, he would still have the same effect on her. An intense effect. That he'd still be raising all the feelings he was raising in her right now.

Because it wasn't the eighteen- or nineteen- or twenty-year-old Clint she was itching to be with again tonight.

It was the present-day Clint. The all-grown-up Clint. The man.

And if the feelings that were emerging for him were shadowed by feelings she'd had for him long ago, feelings that hadn't ever truly disappeared?

Shadows were all they were.

Because when she sorted them out she realized that most of the feelings she had for him at that moment were new. Most of them were inspired by the Clint of today.

And all of them were even stronger than anything she'd felt for him fifteen years ago.

It unnerved her to discover that suddenly.

But it was true.

Maybe it had something to do with the fact that fifteen years ago there'd been a part of her that had held her feelings in check, thinking that her time with him was only temporary, that as soon as Ivey graduated high school the romance with Clint would have to come to an end so Savannah and Ivey could leave Elk Creek and their father.

Maybe her feelings then had just been less mature. The feelings of a teenager. A teenager with an unhappy home life that took precedence over everything else.

But for whatever the reason, her feelings for Clint now were more powerful. More all-consuming. More potent.

And if she'd thought she loved him then, what did that make these feelings now?

Did she love him?

The answer to that scared her.

It scared her so much she almost wished she hadn't

come back here. That she hadn't met up with Clint again at all.

Because in spite of having fought it. In spite of having tried to resist him, there was a very real chance that she did love Clint Culhane.

In the here and now.

She just didn't know what to do with that fact.

Or if she could do anything with it.

Or if it made any difference to anything or anyone.

Anyone but her.

What would she do if she had to take these feelings back to Cheyenne with her and try to bury them the way she'd buried the feelings she'd left with fifteen years ago? How would she survive if those feelings turned out to be one-sided?

She tried hard to bury the feelings right then. To push down on them. To make them go away. But they were resilient little devils that resisted her every attempt. And it occurred to her that not only were the feelings stronger now—her defenses against them were weaker.

And that meant that she was probably in trouble.

Big, big trouble....

The small boutique in Elk Creek had yielded Savannah the quintessential little black dress for the homecoming dance. It was elegant in the simplicity of its round neck, cap sleeves, and short—very short—length. And it hugged every inch of her body like the whisper of a summer's breeze.

Since there wasn't to be any formality to Ivey and Cully's wedding and they'd already had enough dinners to celebrate, they had decided against a rehearsal dinner on this, the eve of their wedding. They'd thought to go to the homecoming dance instead. But that afternoon they'd opted for changing those plans, too, in order to have an evening by themselves.

So, while Ivey waited for Cully, she concentrated on helping Savannah get ready.

The younger sister had persuaded the older to finally buy mascara and blush in shades better suited for her, and Ivey experimented with Savannah's hair, trying for an upswept affair.

But the tomboy-of-old in Savannah couldn't go quite that far, and in the end she brushed it out and left her hair the way she always wore it—long, loose, naturally free around her face and shoulders.

Three-inch heels and lip gloss with the faintest hint of color to it were the last touches, and then Savannah went downstairs where Ivey had gone moments before to let Cully in.

Clint wasn't far behind his brother, driving up outside just as Cully was giving his stamp of approval to Savannah's appearance.

"Ol' Clint's all duded up, too," Cully announced as Savannah opened the door to the only Culhane she had eyes for.

"All duded up" meant Clint had on a pair of gray slacks that no Savile Row tailor could have made fit any better; a crisp, blindingly white Western dress shirt with pearl snaps down the front; and a black string tie held together with a small silver *CC*—one *C* slightly above the other and connected to the second—the cattle brand for the Culhane ranch.

He was freshly showered and shaved, his hair was

combed, and altogether he was a sight to take Savannah's breath away.

Apparently he thought as well of her efforts because he let his gaze do a slow roll from top to toe and back again, commenting with a soft, appreciative whistle on the return trip.

"You look good enough to make my mouth water," he said when he was finished looking her over.

Savannah did something totally unlike herself at that. She spun around to show off, even as the tomboy in her sat back in amazement.

But she felt very feminine tonight. Feminine and excited for a taste of what she'd been denied as a young girl.

Not to mention excited to be with Clint again.

He'd opened the screen door when she'd opened the paneled one but he hadn't come across the threshold yet. And he didn't now. He merely held his hand out to her and said, "Let's get to this dance so I have some justification."

"Justification for what?"

"For bein' up close and personal to what I'm feastin' my eyes on," he said with a wicked wink that took the silliness out of the sound of what he'd said.

But it was a sentiment she wholly agreed with, so she took the hand he offered, said good-night to Ivey and Cully, who looked on like two doting parents, and let Clint lead her to his truck.

To the driver's side again, clearly letting her know he didn't want her sitting all the way over on the passenger's side.

Not that she wanted to herself, so without commenting on it, she slid only to the center of the truck's bench seat before Clint climbed behind the wheel.

"We got called an old habit today at Ivey's wedding shower," she told him as he headed down the drive.

"By who?"

"Nancy Dray. I understand she has her cap set for you." Savannah managed to conceal the fact that it made her jealous, and instead sounded as if she were only razzing him.

"Oh, don't I know it." He answered as if just the thought annoyed him. "She thinks she can lead me to the altar with a trail of home cookin'." He shot a quick glance at Savannah before returning his eyes to the road. "But she's wrong. Nothin' she makes tastes *that* good."

"Mmm," Savannah said as if she wasn't sure she believed him.

"Besides," he added with a sly smile. "She doesn't have a chance against an old habit. You know how hard they are to break—some of 'em just won't let you be."

"I beg your pardon," Savannah said, pretending offense. "As I recall, it wasn't me who came after you. It was you who came after me."

He nudged her shoulder with his. "Tell the truth now," he goaded, "you know you still aren't over me."

"I beg your pardon," she repeated, pretending more affront.

"Well, you know, you can change your hair, you can change your clothes, but you can't change what's inside."

"That's true enough. I couldn't make myself wear girly hair tonight when Ivey did it up that way. But that doesn't have anything to do with this."

"Sure does." He leaned sideways on the seat and confided, "We're still lightin' the same fires, you and I. And you know what the remedy to yours is, don't you?"

"What?"

"Me. 'Cause you still aren't over me," he repeated as if the thought delighted him even if he was only teasing.

Savannah couldn't help laughing at his exaggerated show of ego. But it was all in fun, so she gave as good as she got. "I think it's you who still isn't over me."

"Guilty as charged," he answered without hesitation as he parked the truck in the school lot. "Guilty as charged. Now let's get into this dance."

He hopped out of the truck like a randy buck and took Savannah's hand to pull her after him into the cool night air. But even without a coat she didn't feel the chill. Not when his words had left her with a rosy glow that warmed her from the inside out. And it didn't hurt anything that he kept hold of her hand as they went in.

Since the total high school enrollment was only eighty students for grades nine through twelve, a lot of townsfolk filled in the spare ranks of the gym Savannah and Clint had helped decorate for the occasion. The gym lights were left off, and several spotlights from the drama department had been brought in and rigged with rotating wheels that threw spots of color all along the ceiling, floor, walls and dancers.

Savannah and Clint said hello to a number of people as they worked their way into the room, and then the music of a small band hired from a neighboring town began, and Clint asked Savannah to dance.

"I'm pretty rusty," she cautioned as they stepped into the center of the gym floor. "Remember that night out in the open field, when we danced to the music playing on your truck radio fifteen years ago? That was my last time."

"No," he said in disbelief.

"Yes," she confirmed ominously.

"I think we'll do okay, anyway," Clint said with some self-assurance as he swung her into his arms.

The self-assurance wasn't without merit.

He was even more smooth and graceful than he'd been out in that field. Smooth and graceful enough for the two of them, leading her so effortlessly it made her feel almost adept.

"You're pretty good at this," she told him with a glance up at his handsome face a few minutes into that first dance. "Better even than before."

"I've had some practice. Not a lot to do around here but go to dances," he countered, dipping her with a bit of flourish that made her laugh the way he'd intended her to.

Savannah didn't want to think about all the women he'd had practice with over the years, so she just concentrated on the dance and Clint, reveling in being in his arms, being led around the dance floor as if they were gliding on air.

There was something soothing about dancing. Something so relaxing that Savannah began to understand how people could do it far into the night.

But they didn't get that chance. Unfortunately, after about an hour of slow songs, the teenagers complained and the tempo of the music picked up. So did the noise level, and to escape it Clint suggested a walk through the school.

The halls were quiet, dimly lit and dotted here and there with more teenagers who apparently didn't give a hoot about the music, fast or slow, because they'd come to pair up for some intense kissing in the relative privacy of the deserted corridors.

Clint held Savannah's hand again but that seemed pretty tame next to some of the couples they passed.

Nodding in the direction of two teenagers in a clinch that had them nearly inside an open locker, she said, "So who did you kiss in the halls when we were kids?"

"During school or during school dances?"

"Both."

"You want the whole list?"

"It must be a long one."

"What if I told you that I never enjoyed kissin' any of 'em as much as I would have enjoyed kissin' you, if only I'd noticed you before the last week of our senior year?"

"I'd say bull!"

Clint laughed. "Well, you'd be wrong."

She wanted him to prove it. To stop their leisurely stroll and kiss her there in the hall, just to see what it would have been like.... Well, that and just to have him kiss her.

But he didn't do it.

Then, as if he knew what she was thinking, he explained why not. "Trouble with kissin' here in the halls is that you get all het up and hot and bothered and the only place to take it is into the bathroom or the janitor's room or some other spot that's uncomfortable and prone to somebody else walkin' in on you.''

''Spoken like a man who knows from experience,'' she goaded again.

But he didn't expand on it. He just said, ''Watch,'' and flung open a supply closet door to expose yet another couple in a more passionate embrace than those in the corridors.

Then, sounding for all the world as if he hadn't known exactly what he was doing, he said, ''Sorry,'' and closed the door again. But he was grinning from ear to ear, enjoying his bit of orneriness.

''How did you know there was somebody in there?'' she asked with a laugh as they walked on.

''Good guess.''

''Because it was probably your favorite spot.''

He just went on grinning. ''Think so?''

''I think you're incorrigible, is what I think.''

''I think I heard another slow song comin' from the gym,'' he said, taking her hand to lead her back.

For some reason the tone of the evening changed after that, as if the young romances going on out in the hallways had infected them. Or maybe the open show of affection had just knocked down what little reserves they'd been hanging on to before.

But from then on—fast song or slow—Clint and Savannah used the excuse of dancing to be in each other's arms.

And it was just an excuse, because they really only stayed in one corner, barely moving to the music, completely out of sync with the loud, frenetic rock and roll, or head-banging heavy-metal songs that were played periodically to keep everybody happy.

But Savannah wouldn't have had it any other way.

Because something happened as they swayed there together all that time. Things began to fall away for her. Worries about the past, the present, the future. Inhibitions. The whole of the fifteen years that had separated them.

And what was left was a new closeness. A new connection to go with the new feelings she'd realized she had for him earlier in the day. A rediscovery of the sense that they were two halves of a whole—even if that realization unnerved her.

They didn't talk much. They didn't need to. Not even changes in the music penetrated the cocoon that seemed to wrap them, cushion them from anything outside of each other's arms.

Savannah's head rested in the hollow of Clint's shoulder as if that spot had been specially fashioned for her. He laid his cheek against her hair, and that was how they stayed. Swaying. Holding each other. Lost in a world all their own.

And when the band announced the last dance of the evening, Savannah could hardly believe it was already midnight.

"The PTA has a candlelight supper set up in the cafeteria," Clint said as they remained the way they were for that final dance. "Are you hungry?"

Not for food. Or for people intruding on the solitude they'd somehow found even in the midst of the crowd.

Savannah looked up at him. "Are you?" she countered.

"Not enough to let go of you."

"Me, neither."

"Have any better ideas?"

Savannah knew what he was doing. Tonight he was leaving it up to her as to how their evening ended.

It was only fair since she'd cut short what had been happening between them the night before, because she'd had reservations. And so she gave some thought to how to answer his question about where to go from there.

Not that it took too much thought.

Regardless of what had gone through her mind to keep her from making love with him the previous evening, standing there in his arms now, she couldn't think of a single reason not to let nature take the course it was crying out to take. She couldn't think of a single reason strong enough to mar the perfection of their being together.

She wanted him. Wanted to be with him in the most intimate way she could. And suddenly nothing else seemed as important as that.

"There's no place for us to be alone," she said, lamenting that fact out loud. "Cully and Ivey are at my house. Yance and the kids are at yours...."

Clint smiled down at her. "Bein' alone isn't a problem. I know where we can go for that."

The unspoken part, though, was his wondering if the problem would be Savannah being uncertain about this the way she'd been the night before.

But she didn't need to think any more about it. She'd made up her mind.

"Show me" was all she said.

Clint studied her closely for a while, searching her eyes with his as if to be certain himself. He still didn't seem totally convinced when he said, "Let's go then," and, holding her hand once more, he led her out to the truck.

But even once they'd reached it, neither of them seemed inclined to disconnect, so Savannah sat close to him on the bench seat, intensely aware of even small details—like the way his big, capable hand rested on the steering wheel, controlling it without much effort; like the way her shoulder found just the right spot nestled into his side; like the spread of his thighs and the juncture where they met....

His other arm stayed around her, that hand rubbing her elbow as she used his shoulder as a pillow for her head. She breathed in the mingling scents of his aftershave and her perfume, blending so well into a clean, spicy mixture that it seemed the one was supposed to go with the other just to make her head light.

He drove past her house and pulled into the drive that led to his place farther down the road. But he didn't stop there. Instead he kept on going to a small outbuilding behind the Culhanes' main ranch house.

It was a single, square cottage that hadn't existed fifteen years ago, set far back, away from the other structures in a copse of trees. It looked like an adult-size dollhouse, its whitewashed siding trimmed in pale yellow and dripping with gingerbread that hung from eaves forming a peak above the front door.

"What's this?" Savannah asked as he pulled to a stop in front of it and turned off the engine.

"We call it the honeymoon hut. Mostly we use it

as a guest house now. Or when one of us gets ticked off at the rest and needs some time out for some reason. But Yance and I built it for Cully when he married Amy and Randa's mother. It was damn near painful to be two bachelors in the same house with a pair of newlyweds, so we put up this place for their privacy and our peace of mind."

"It's great."

"It might be a little dusty but it shouldn't be too bad. We had some of our family in from out of town use it a few weeks ago."

Yet even with that said he didn't make a move to get out of the truck. Instead he angled more toward Savannah and looked down into her eyes once more. "Don't let me go in there and then change your mind," he warned...or beseeched, really.

"I'm not going to change my mind," she said without having to think about it.

There was nothing *to* think about. At that moment there wasn't a single thing she'd ever wanted as much as she wanted to spend the night with him in that quaint cottage. And nothing that had come before, nothing that would come after, mattered more to her right then than that she have this small space in time to herself, without thoughts of anything but the two of them. Together again....

Clint took her at her word and finally got out of the truck, keeping hold of her hand still and taking her with him up onto the tiny porch that sat like a saucer around a teacup.

The honeymoon hut wasn't locked so he merely opened the door, reached in to flip on a light and let Savannah enter ahead of him.

Inside it was like a studio apartment—one room with a small kitchenette and a single sofa facing a portable television on the right side. In the rear, through an open doorway, Savannah could see an enclosed bathroom complete with a tub large enough for two. On the other side of the room was a night table and lamp beside a very big bed covered in a fluffy, inviting quilt.

Clint had been right—there was a little dust dimming the hard surfaces, but not much. Just enough to let Savannah know that he hadn't planned this and come to spruce it up in anticipation. She appreciated that he hadn't been that sure of her or of himself or of how this evening might end.

"What do you think?" he asked from behind her, the door still open and his voice sounding a little cautious as if testing to see if she might be having second thoughts after all.

Savannah turned to look at him, smiling, her heart full of feelings for him. "I think I'm very glad to be here with you," she admitted.

He finally seemed to accept that because the questioning frown on his brow smoothed out and was replaced by enough of a smile to draw those creases down his cheeks.

He took a few backward steps in order to slam the door shut, still holding her hand and letting their arms extend between them. But he didn't rush right back. Instead he studied her from that distance for a moment, as if he couldn't quite believe she was real

Then he let go of her hand and slowly began another approach toward her, this with an obviously more intimate intent as the air seemed to crackle with sensual tension all of a sudden.

Savannah watched him come nearer, watched him lean in, bending enough to press his lips against hers, but she didn't so much as raise her chin to meet him. Not at first. She stayed the way she was, where she was, as he dipped down.

But when he kissed her again she couldn't help tilting her face just a little to accommodate him. To drink the nectar of his lips the way he drank the nectar of hers. Without touching her. Only letting their mouths meet.

Until the third kiss.

The third kiss was the charm.

He slid one hand into her hair to her nape, the other slipped under her arm to her back to pull her up close to him.

Savannah reached instinctively for his arms—big, muscled arms that her palms climbed, following the bulge of his biceps, his deltoids, curving over his shoulders to the taut trapezius muscles until she found the thick, strong column of his neck, until her fingertips teased the slightly long hair that waved above his shirt collar.

It felt so good to touch him. So good she had to backtrack just so she could take that trip again, savoring the feel of the power and strength contained in arms so big her hands couldn't even begin to span them. And each trip set off an electrical current that shot through her palms into her own arms, charging them, charging her whole body with a sensual appreciation, arousing a yearning to have even the thin cloth of his shirtsleeves out of the way so she could test the warmth of his skin without the hindrance of it.

He led her a few steps nearer the bed.

But, as if the distance was too great to cover without stopping for the sustenance of another kiss, he paused to pull her playfully, forcefully, into his embrace again. Against his body, his hands encircling her waist, riding high enough for the tips of his thumbs to barely brush the bottommost curves of her breasts.

It was only a taste of things to come, though, before those wonderful hands retreated. Before his mouth left hers. Before he took her hand and led her the rest of the way to the bed to stop beside it.

Once more he kissed her. Or maybe she kissed him. It was difficult to tell because they came together at the same instant. Hungry. Urgent. Almost frantic to touch each other. To kiss each other. Not to be parted for even a moment.

Their bodies met as if they'd been carved from the same stone so that for every outcropping there was a nook, for every nook, the perfect outcropping. Melding together as if they really were made for each other.

Tongues played, searched, joined them and then pulled free as Clint seemed to force his head up and away from hers even as he held her cheeks cupped in his hands.

"I want you, Savannah," he said, his breath a hot gust only inches from her face. "I never stopped wanting you." He smiled down at her once more. And then, as if the floodgates had been opened, he captured her lips with his yet again. More urgently than ever before.

She heard, rather than felt, the zipper of her dress go down, and it made her laugh slightly beneath the magic of his mouth.

But only in delight, in pleasure at the fact that he finally intended to rid them of some of the clothes that barred them from the closeness she craved.

And she meant to rid them of even more, so she went to work on the snaps of his shirt even as she tugged the tails out of his slacks.

Hurrying, hurrying, she nearly tore his shirt off, hungry to fill her hands with the silken feel of his bare torso. With the warm sleekness of flesh over firm muscle.

He took care of the rest. Of his clothes and hers, letting everything fall around her ankles to be kicked away, and leaving her completely bare to his admiring gaze as he dropped what remained of his own clothing, too.

"You're even more beautiful now than you were all those years ago," he breathed as he flung back the quilt to expose crisp white sheets and eased her backward onto the mattress.

They were apart just long enough for her to sneak a quick peek at his body, too. Long enough to see that his was definitely not the body of a boy just maturing, the way it had been when they'd last made love.

No, this was the body of a full-grown man. Honed and refined. Work-carved and chiseled. Gloriously, masculinely beautiful.

And hard with wanting her.

But even though she could have gone on looking at him forever, when he kissed her again, it aroused too much in her for her to keep her eyes open for long. Magnificent as he was to behold, she didn't want anything to distract her, to keep her from succumbing to the pure delights of the feelings coursing through her.

Clint toyed with her hair, following a long strand of it between his fingers to where it fell past her shoulder, past her collarbone to the top swell of her breast.

Again he barely brushed the sensitive mound but it was enough to tighten her nipple into a hard knot that strained for so much more.

Her back arched all on its own, giving a silent message of what she wanted, what she needed, what she craved.

And finally he gave it. One of those incredible hands covered her breast. Firmly. Completely. Encasing it in a toughened palm that was so gentle, so tender, so talented...

Kneading, massaging, toying with her breast, he took his time. Learned every inch, teased and tormented until she was writhing beneath his masterful touch. Until her nipple almost ached, until a tight cord seemed to stretch from that spot to one much lower, between her legs.

He stopped kissing her then. Her lips, at least. Instead he kissed his way along the column of her neck to her shoulder and then downward, reaching her breast with the warm, moist velvet of his mouth. Suckling, flicking his tongue against the engorged crest, circling it, driving her out of her mind with the sharp shards of light that erupted inside her, with the desire for more…more…

He ran a flattened palm down her stomach and lower still, reaching that already ignited core between her legs, exploring, searching, finding the center of her with gentle pressure and seeking fingers that made her moan beneath the intensity of the sensations only he could arouse.

A driving need suddenly sprang to life within her, to touch him, to feel him, to do to him the wild and wonderful things he was doing to her.

And so she took one of her hands from where they both pressed against the broad expanse of his back, sliding it around to his pectorals, discovering his own male nibs almost as hard as her nipples were.

But she didn't linger long there. Not when she had something else in mind. Something so much better to seek out.

She reveled in the flat washboard of his belly, in the tautness of his hips, and then she found what she sought. The long, steely hardness of his desire for her.

This time it was Clint who moaned in a deep, delicious agony of delight as her hand closed around him, as she did some exploring of her own, as she put into play just the right pressure, just the right motion to drive him as wonderfully insane with desire as he was driving her.

Until neither of them could bear it any longer.

Clint's mouth deserted her breast, coming back to capture her lips in a wide-open kiss, plunging his tongue in at the same moment that he rose above her, eased his weight onto her and eased himself into her. Inch by inch. Slowly he found his way home, entering her completely, filling the emptiness of her, completing her.

He moaned as if he'd found heaven inside her, just before he pulled out slightly, then plunged in again, thrusting with a rhythm that matched her heartbeat. Gaining speed and intensity as need mounted, he began to race, hard and fast as Savannah clung to him, met him thrust for thrust, raising her hips toward him, accepting the fullness of him as deeply inside her as she possibly could.

Together they climbed the mountain of that impeccable union in a melding of not only their bodies but their hearts and souls, too.

Climbing, straining, striving...

Savannah reached the peak ahead of him, bursting through the clouds into a white-hot ecstasy that racked every fiber of her being, that took her soaring, soaring, higher and higher, that seemed to stop her breathing, stop her pulse, stop everything for one blindingly exquisite moment before it began to ebb, to carry her back to earth, to leave her soft and yielding as Clint, too, found his climax and embedded himself into the deepest center of her, filling her, holding her, branding her as his own.

And then taut, tense muscles eased. Bodies relaxed, and Clint became a divine heaviness atop her as he breathed hot air into her hair and kissed the top of her head with a sweet tenderness that seemed to seal things between them.

For a few moments, Savannah wondered if anything could be more perfect than what they'd just shared.

And yet, as Clint kissed her one more time before

settling into an exhausted slumber, other feelings suddenly seeped in.

Feelings that were strange to have right then. Feelings that brought to mind things she didn't want to think about. Things like that miscarriage she'd had fifteen years ago and the secret she'd kept from Clint until only recently.

It was guilt that was rushing through her, she realized when she examined the feelings more closely.

Guilt and something else....

Something that seemed a whole lot as if she'd just received a gift she didn't deserve.

Undeserving. That was it. She felt undeserving.

Undeserving of that moment.

Undeserving of the kind of bliss she'd just found.

But most of all, undeserving of this man....

## Chapter Nine

In the heat of the moment the night before, Clint had forgotten about the heat of the honeymoon hut. Or rather the lack of it, since the thermostat was set on a very low temperature when no one was using the place regularly.

Wrapped in each other's arms, the cold didn't penetrate them until dawn, when he woke to Savannah nuzzling against him in her sleep. He'd have been thrilled with that, except it didn't take long to figure out she was huddling for warmth rather than snuggling for any better, more pleasurable reason.

His first clue was when she poked his chest with a nose so cold it could have been an icicle. His second was when she inched frigid toes under his calf, and by then he knew he had to turn up the heat in spite of the fact that it meant getting out of bed to do it.

Being careful not to wake her, he gently rolled her to her back and eased himself off the mattress. The hardwood floor was none too warm, either, so he light-footed it to the thermostat to rectify the situation, then light-footed it back to bed again.

He slid just as cautiously under the covers when he got there, slipped his arm behind her neck and shoulders and finessed her back to where she'd been before.

Once she was, Savannah made a sound that was almost a purr, did more snuggling until she seemed to find just the right spot against him, and settled once more, all without waking.

Clint didn't even try to go back to sleep, though. Instead he closed his eyes and savored just being there in bed with her. Having her in his arms. Her head on his chest. Her soft breath, her silken hair against his skin. Her hand resting atop his stomach. One leg slung over his thighs now.

If that wasn't heaven on earth he didn't know what was.

Serenity. Contentment. Perfect comfort.

It was as if they were accustomed to sleeping together. As if they'd been doing it every night for years and years.

For fifteen years. The way they should have been.

The way they could be from now on....

When that thought popped into his mind he opened his eyes.

He'd done a lot of pondering on the past. Of testing the waters of the present. But suddenly it didn't seem too far-fetched to consider him and Savannah actually having a future together. Actually spending every night the way they'd spent the last one. Actually waking up every morning like this, with her fitting perfectly at his side.

But he was no young kid anymore, something inside him reminded. He was old enough to know that life wasn't made up only of nights of passion and mornings of cuddling.

What about the day that stretched between? What about the whole spectrum of the life that would lie ahead? Were he and Savannah a good match?

That last was a dumb question, he told himself.

Of course they were a good match. They liked the same things. They had the same values. The same work ethic. They had a great time together. Got along just fine. And genuinely liked each other, unless he was mistaken, but he didn't think she would have given over her whole trip here to him if she didn't like him. And he knew damn well he liked her.

Liked. And loved.

Savannah hadn't said the words, but he knew he hadn't imagined her passion last night. Surely this wasn't just a nostalgic interlude for her.

And that brought him back to the real problem—their past, or more specifically, how that past might affect their future.

Was he seeing the present-day Savannah with a clear eye? The clear eye he'd sworn to use if he ever started to think about making the same commitment to another woman that he'd almost made to Franny.

It was true that Savannah, like Franny, had kept

secrets from him. But Savannah's secrets were different.

Sure, he wished she'd come to him with the news of her pregnancy before telling anyone else. But the mistake of confiding in her sister when she didn't think their father was anywhere around had been just that—a mistake. There hadn't been anything malicious in it. Or anything contrived. Or anything that spoke of a flaw in her. Silas Heller overhearing about the baby had been an accident, plain and simple. Not something Clint could hold against her.

So those hard feelings he'd been having, he realized, weren't aimed at Savannah. They were aimed at her father. And fate. But not at her.

And once the miscarriage had happened? he thought. What about what had gone on from there?

If he put himself in her shoes and looked objectively from her perspective, he could see how she might have thought it was for the best not to tell him. What purpose would it have served?

He couldn't have turned back the clock so that the whole event had never happened. But he had to admit that at the time he'd been a headstrong twenty-year-old. He would have been stark-raving mad at her father on top of never having liked the man and having resented the way he treated Savannah even before. Given that, it was likely he would have gone off half-cocked and done something he shouldn't have. Something that could have had far-reaching consequences.

No, as mad as Clint would have been to find out that the old man had caused Savannah to miscarry, if she'd told him, it would have been like lighting the fuse on a whole case of dynamite.

So in a lot of ways, what she'd done by keeping the secret was to take the burden completely onto herself and make things easier for everyone else.

Easier for her father, who shouldn't have gotten away with what he'd done. But at the same time easier for Ivey to leave Elk Creek the way she and Savannah had planned, the way Ivey probably wouldn't have done on her own. Easier for Clint, who hadn't suffered the grief and rage over the baby, even though he had suffered over losing Savannah.

None of that spoke of the sort of character he needed to avoid. The kind of character Franny had had. Or had lacked. It spoke of the kind of character he wanted in a wife. In the mother of his children. Especially when there was nothing about Savannah that was secretive—other than that single incident when not telling him what had happened had safeguarded everyone but her.

But what about those periodic hard feelings he kept having? he asked himself. Even if they weren't aimed at Savannah, would they shade any future the two of them might be able to share?

He couldn't deny that he had them. It hurt him to think about what might have been. To wonder if he'd have had a daughter or a son. What she or he would be like now.

But it *was* all in the past, he reminded himself. Long past. And there was no more he could do about it now than he could have done about it fifteen years ago. Nothing would be accomplished by dwelling on it. By sacrificing this new relationship he and Savannah had begun. By not letting it go forward the way he wanted it to. By denying them both what they had together.

In fact, it occurred to him that making a happy future with Savannah might sap some of the power out of the regrets for what might have been. That building what they should have been able to build then, having kids, might have some power in healing the hurt over the child they'd lost, over the missed years.

No, the more he thought about it, the more convinced he was that a happy future with Savannah now could go a long way in making up for the past.

Because the truth was, the hurts and hard feelings were nothing compared to the soft feelings he had for her at that moment, with her in his arms. They were nothing compared to the feelings he had every minute he'd been with her since she'd come back to Elk Creek.

The bottom line was that nothing could hold a candle to how much he loved her. Because, man, did he love her! With every ounce of his being.

And as for the days that stretched between mornings waking up with her in his arms and nights like the last one? As for the whole spectrum of life that stretched out ahead of him?

There wasn't anyone on the face of the earth he'd rather spend any of that time with than Savannah.

So would the past affect their future together? he asked himself once and for all.

Yes, if it kept them apart. If he let the past ruin

what they could have together right now. Because he didn't doubt that he saw Savannah with a clear eye. And what he saw was the only woman he'd ever truly loved. The only woman he *would* ever truly love.

The woman he knew without a doubt that he was supposed to be with.

And come hell or high water, he meant to be with her.

Forever from this day forward.

As long as she wanted him, too....

There were a couple of things that woke Savannah up.

Her cold nose for one. Nuzzled to something wonderfully warm.

Her cold toes for another. Entwined with what felt like hot, hairy legs.

And a kid-leather-textured hand rubbing lightly, tenderly, sensually up and down her back.

She had a vague memory of falling asleep the night before with some disturbing feelings running through her. But in that particular moment of weighted, lazy waking, when her senses were more in command than her brain was, the memory was so vague it didn't seem anywhere near as important as what Clint was rousing in her.

"Mmm," she said, having meant to say *morning* but incapable of more than the moan of pleasure.

"You awake?" he asked with a smile in his voice, knowing full well he was ensuring she wasn't sleeping any longer with every stroke of that hand.

But Savannah only muttered another, "Mmm," in

answer, her eyes still closed, rubbing his chest with her cheek where she had used the hard expanse as a pillow.

"I have some things I want to talk to you about," he said, but his tone was too husky to take seriously. Especially when that hand wasn't at her back anymore but had moved to her side to graze the outer bulge of her breast on each upward trek and her hip on each downward one.

"Umm-hmm," she muttered by way of acknowledgment.

Savannah finally opened her eyes so she could tuck in her chin and draw a circle around his nipple with her cold nose. The male nib knotted almost immediately. Which was only fair since both of hers were kerneled and anxious for some attention of their own.

"But maybe talkin' can wait a bit," he said with a deep-throated chuckle when she slid her hand low on his flat belly—not to anything important, but low enough to tease with good effect.

He let out a feral growl when she didn't do more, rolled to his side—taking her with him—and slung a heavy thigh over her to pin her up against him. Face-to-face. Chest to breasts. Belly to belly. Soft pelvis to much, much harder masculine proof of his intent.

"Well, good morning to you, too," she said with a laugh when he flexed that steely shaft against her in sexy greeting.

"Mmm," was all he responded, mimicking her just before he covered her mouth with his in a playful, passionate, openmouthed kiss that wasted no time getting down to business.

Not that Savannah had any complaint with that.

She opened her mouth, too, to welcome him, to meet his seeking, searching tongue and give tit for tat in the game of thrust and parry he seemed to want to play.

His arms were long enough to wrap her in a bear hug that left a hand alongside each of her breasts, his fingertips brushing the very edges of her nipples. Just enough to tantalize her with only a taste of better things to come.

While she waited for those better things she filled her palms with the satin-encased muscles of his back, massaging rolling hills, dipping into the canyon of his spine, sliding into the valley at the base of it and climbing to the raised tautness of a derriere that felt even better than it looked.

She squeezed a little and he answered with another moan, another flex of his manhood against her and a tearing away of his mouth over hers to slide down and capture one straining, craving breast with that warm wetness.

There was urgency already in every movement, in every flick of his tongue against her nipple, every sucking in, every tiny tug of gentle teeth, until Savannah was nearly driven out of her mind with wanting more from him. With the gaping emptiness between her legs that made her feel as if she were incomplete without his body filling hers.

There wasn't much she could do but writhe beneath the magic ministering of his mouth, because he still had her encased in his strong arms—now around her waist, holding on tight.

Not much she could do with her hands, at any rate, but delve into the glory of his back.

One foot was flat against a thick, corded calf, though, and she let it climb, let her knee caress the inside of his thigh until it reached higher, higher, high enough to find a place in the juncture of his legs.

She drew her knee forward. Then backward. Then forward again. Slowly. Carefully. Creatively.

Until he yanked away from her breast with even more fierceness than he'd abandoned her mouth, throwing his head back as if he could hardly bear what she was doing to him.

And then he pressed her the rest of the way to the mattress and rose up above her, spreading her thighs with his, finding his spot between them.

And it *was* his spot. Only his, Savannah thought as she opened to him, willed him to hurry because she couldn't wait to have him inside her.

He sought that moist, yearning entrance of her body with his and eased himself in to fill that aching need she'd been trying to convey, trying to raise to the same level in him.

Apparently she'd succeeded, because from the start he dove deeply into her, plunging to her core, pulling out only to drive in again and again at a tempo too fast, too intense for her to match.

Savannah could only cling to him and give herself completely over to his mastery, letting him take her on the wild ride he was bent on running. It was as if they were racing through time, through space. Soaring through air, unfettered to anything but each other.

With perfect rhythm, perfect rise and fall, perfect

pace and pressure, power and passion, he brought her headlong into a climax that shot through her like white lightning. That arched her spine. That nearly brought her off the bed. That dug her fingers into his back. That forced tiny, high-pitched sounds from her throat. That went on and on, taking her further and further into a realm of pleasure she hadn't even reached the night before, holding her at that peak for a blinding few minutes so intense, so incredible, so exquisite she wanted it to go on and on, never to end, never...

But nothing that glorious could last indefinitely, and only when it began to ebb did she realize Clint was reaching his own destination, poised over her, inside of her, frozen in a culmination that seemed to turn him to stone—hard, solid, divinely carved stone—until he shuddered, pushed even farther into her than she thought was possible, and finally began to breathe again. Heavy breaths as he let arms that had been holding him in a locked-elbow push-up relax and lower him more completely on top of her.

When he had he pulsed inside her. Once. Twice. Three times. In a way that tickled her from the inside out and almost brought her to a second, sudden, unexpected peak before her exhausted body did a slight shudder of its own and succumbed to a warm afterglow that seemed to mesh their bodies together at every curve, every swell—that gave her the sense that they really were melded into one.

"Guess we heated this place up, all right," Clint said in a raspy, passion-ragged voice when they'd both begun to breathe normally again.

"My nose and toes are definitely warm now," she agreed.

He raised up enough to rub the tip of his nose against hers in what they'd called Eskimo kisses as kids. "Feels warm to me," he confirmed.

Then he rolled them both into the position they'd awakened in—Clint on his back, one arm around Savannah, Savannah lying at his side, her head on his chest.

"I love you, Savannah," he said then, sounding much more serious.

"I love you, too," she answered, a question in her tone about why he'd changed suddenly. "Is that what you wanted to talk about?"

"What I wanted to talk about was us gettin' married the way we should have fifteen years ago."

Savannah went cold again. But this time it had nothing to do with the temperature in the honeymoon cottage. And it wasn't only her nose and toes that turned instantly frigid. This chilled her to the bone.

"I want you to marry me," he repeated. "And I want us to have that baby we should have had. Right away."

She rolled from him and sat up, pulling the sheet to cover herself. But somehow she still felt too exposed. Too vulnerable. And she ended up getting out of bed with the sheet wrapped around her toga fashion.

"I...I have to go to the bathroom," was all she could think to say, grabbing up her clothes as she went and hurrying for the seclusion of the other room.

Of the barrier of the door she closed between herself and Clint.

What she wanted to do, what every instinct she had was urging her to do, was run. Out of the cottage. Out of Elk Creek. As far away from Clint and that proposal as she could go.

But why? she asked herself, when she caught sight of her own reflection in the mirror over the sink and was shocked to find herself looking like a doe caught in headlights. Why had Clint's proposal put her into such a tailspin?

She did love him, heaven help her. Hadn't she fantasized just a night or two before about having the life they'd talked about as kids? About being his wife? About having his children?

But that was all it had been—a fantasy, another voice inside her head argued. It wasn't real.

*Real* was an enraged father. *Real* was a baby lost because she hadn't been careful enough. *Real* was living with that fact for fifteen years.

*Real* wasn't this quaint little cottage in this quaint small town where happily ever after seemed the order of the day. That might be real for other people. It might be real for Ivey. But it wasn't the reality for Savannah. Not with all that water under the bridge....

She dropped the sheet from around her and began to pull on her clothes with shaking, almost frenzied fingers.

*Real* wasn't marrying Clint and pretending nothing bad had kept them apart all this time, that little voice continued to say as she dressed. *Real* wasn't just having other babies as if the one she'd lost hadn't meant anything. To do any of that was to try living in the fantasy. And Savannah wasn't the kind of person to ever think that could be done.

By the time she had finished dressing and screwed up the courage to leave the bathroom, she thought she had a good grip on things. On herself. On what reality was. On what reality wasn't. And on what she had to do.

It was just difficult to keep hold of it when she set eyes on Clint again.

He'd gotten out of bed, too, and pulled on his shirt and slacks from the night before. But the shirt wasn't buttoned or tucked in. It hung loosely around his hips, open down the front and leaving her facing the magnificence of that broad, amazingly developed chest and rock-hard belly.

The sight of that, of the morning shadow of his beard making him look rugged and masculine and all the more handsome, of his finger combed hair and those penetrating—albeit troubled—blue eyes, made her weak-kneed. And it didn't help that she felt as if he'd left his imprint on her body, as if she could still feel him on top of her, inside her, wrapped around her, and how wonderful that had been.

But she pushed all that out of her mind and worked to keep herself focused on those realities she'd reminded herself of in the bathroom.

"So," Clint said, keeping a close eye on her. "I thought this was goin' pretty well until the answer to my askin' you to marry me was 'I have to go to the bathroom.'"

He was trying to lighten the tension that had de-

scended on the honeymoon cottage with her rush out
of the room. But it was a feeble attempt, and he barely
managed a hint of a smile before his features settled
into a confused frown.

"Was I wrong?" he asked when she didn't say
anything.

"We've been having a good time," Savannah said,
hedging.

"We've been having more than that."

"Clint—"

"Don't try to tell me what we've shared since
hooking up again has just been a good time—as if
there was nothing else to it. We both know that's a
lie."

"Okay. It's a lie. But—"

"But what? Has it meant more to me than it has
to you? I said I love you and that's the God's honest
truth. You said you loved me. Was that a lie, too?"

"No," she said quickly, unable to let him think
that, even if it wouldn't matter in the end.

"Seems to me that two people who love each
other—two people who've loved each other for the
better part of their lives—should be together. Should
grab for their second chance. Should grab for the opportunity to make up for the past. To heal the hurts
and make right what went wrong."

Savannah shook her head. Fiercely. "You can't rewrite history, Clint. No new babies will ever be able
to wipe away what happened. They'd never be able
to make up for losing that baby we might have had
so many years ago."

"I know that. And I'm not tryin' to rewrite history.

I'm tryin' to start now what should have started then. Late, yeah, but what we have together is every bit as—maybe even more—potent than what we had before. We *love* each other, Savannah. We deserve to have a life together.''

*Deserve…*

That was what she'd fallen to sleep thinking about the previous night—that she didn't deserve Clint or the happiness she found with him or all he could make her feel. The memory she'd awakened with wasn't vague anymore. And neither was the feeling. It came back full force with just his saying that word.

''You know, I'm not that different from the woman you almost married before,'' she said, because it seemed like the best way to prove to him that this wasn't going to work out for them.

''Because you kept the fact that you'd lost the baby a secret from me the way she kept her past a secret? I've thought about that and it's malarkey. She was covering up lousy things she'd done. Lousy things I needed to know to understand what kind of person she was. But you—''

''Covered up something lousy I did.''

''What did you do? You told Ivey about the pregnancy. What happened with your father is on his head. You were as much the victim as the baby was.''

''I wasn't a victim. I was responsible for that life. For what ended it.''

''That's crazy.''

''It isn't crazy. The same way that Franny person didn't protect her child from the boyfriend who abused it, I didn't protect our baby from my father.''

"You were a kid. A scared kid—"

"That's no excuse. There are no excuses that change the facts."

"Savannah—"

"No. You want to just go back, as if our getting married now will make the rest disappear from the history books. But it won't change what went on. What I *let* go on."

"All right," he conceded, but he didn't seem to agree; he only seemed to be humoring her. "We can't make anything disappear from the history books. We can't bring back the fifteen years or the baby we lost. But that doesn't mean we can't have a future together."

Except that she didn't deserve to....

"It just wouldn't work for me," she said.

"Why not?"

"Coming back here. Marrying you. Going on as if that baby hadn't died...I just can't do that."

"Why not?" he shouted in frustration, flinging his hands in the air.

"Because I couldn't live with myself."

"People make mistakes, Savannah. Kids, especially, make mistakes—and we were just kids. That doesn't mean you have to pay for it for the rest of your life. It doesn't mean you can't *have* a life. Or love. Or happiness. It doesn't mean we can't be together now."

"It does for me," she said very, very quietly because reality, for her, was tearing her apart inside.

"I should never have come back here," she muttered more to herself than to him.

"We lost a baby," Clint said then, calm again, his deep, rich voice soothing. "But we still love each other and we can go forward from here. Make a new stab at a life together. Maybe gettin' married, havin' other babies would make up for the one that didn't get to be. It might not take away any of what happened or how we feel about it, but it would be makin' somethin' good and decent out of what we feel for each other. Feelin's that made that baby in the first place. How can that be wrong?"

Oh, Lord, but it was tempting.

Clint was tempting.

There he was, more handsome than she could believe. Kind. Sweet. A man with no equal in her eyes. A man she loved so much it hurt.

And part of her screamed for her to forget the past. To latch on to the future he was offering and forget everything else.

But she just couldn't do it.

All those feelings from the previous night after they'd made love welled up and joined so many feelings she'd had for the past fifteen years. And she just couldn't do it.

Not when, in her view, it seemed as if she were flagrantly tossing aside the loss of that baby as if it didn't matter. As if it had no more importance than a fly on the wall, swatted into oblivion a decade and a half ago.

She couldn't just pick up where she and Clint had left off and go on as if the baby had never existed. Or as if the events she'd let unfold hadn't.

"No," she said more forcefully, with more finality, shaking her head once again. "I can't marry you."

"You could. If you'd let go of the past."

"Just like that. So what if there was a baby and it died. Forget it. We'll have more."

Clint's expression darkened into a storm cloud of a frown. "That's not what I meant. Do you think it hasn't eaten on me since you told me about the miscarriage? Do you think I haven't pictured our child in every fourteen-year-old I've seen since then? Do you think I haven't wondered if it was a boy or a girl? A daughter or a son? If it would have looked like you or me? Do you think I still couldn't wring your father's neck if he was around now for me to get my hands on him?"

"No," Savannah was quick to say. "I don't think it hasn't bothered you. I know it has. And maybe that's part of why I can't marry you. You're fooling yourself into thinking right now that it wouldn't be there between us."

He looked confused. And frustrated. And it all echoed in his voice and raised the octave it came out in. "Are you sayin' that I'm hidin' some kind of resentment? That I'm holdin' a grudge I just haven't mentioned yet?"

She shrugged slightly. "I'm saying that you haven't lived for very long with knowing about it all. With the feelings it raises and what it's bound to raise the more you think about it. I'm saying that I know from experience that just pushing it out of your mind doesn't make it disappear. Moving out of town, burying yourself in other things, doesn't make it disappear. It has a way of creeping up behind you and making you feel things you don't expect to feel.''

"I love you, Savannah," he said, as if that was the only response he could think of for what she'd said, for the raw pain she knew she was revealing to him in spite of the fact that she'd managed to hide most of it from everyone else for so long. "I hate that somethin' ugly happened to you. I hate that we lost our first child. I hate that we lost fifteen years. I hate that you've carried the burden of this all this time alone. But I'm here to tell you that I don't resent you for any of it. I don't blame you for any of it. And I sure as hell won't start resentin' or blamin' you for it down the road. Whether you're my wife or not.''

"I don't think anybody can say what they might feel down the road.''

"I can. I can tell you I'll love you because I've never stopped. Because I love you more now than I did all that time ago, and I know damn well I'll still be lovin' you when they lay me in my grave. Nothin'—*nothin'*—can change that or turn it sour. I realized that when I realized that even your leavin' town without a word, even your not so much as droppin' me a postcard to tell me why, even findin' out what had run you out of town and about the baby and the miscarriage and the secret you kept that whole time, didn't make me love you any less.''

Her eyes filled up with tears she didn't want to shed. Her heart filled up with love for him. And with pain because she knew that no matter what he said, it didn't change things.

"I just can't," she whispered. "I can't marry you, Clint."

"Savannah—"

"No. I can't. Don't ask me again."

Then she made a run for the door, flung it open and went out into the cool morning air.

But even as she headed across the fallow fields to her own house she didn't feel much of the chill. She didn't feel much of anything except her heart breaking in two.

And all she could think was that she never should have come back to Elk Creek.

That this place was only the site of pain for her. Of anguish. Of loss.

Of loss*es*.

That she should never have come back and rediscovered Clint and her love for him, because now she just had to suffer losing him all over again.

Only this time it actually hurt worse.

Maybe because this time she knew it was **for** good.

## Chapter Ten

Savannah walked through the last-minute prepara-tions for Ivey and Cully's wedding that morning and afternoon like a zombie. A miserable zombie. She didn't confide what had happened between her and Clint to her sister because she didn't want to mar Ivey's happiness on this special day by unloading her own problems on her sister.

It wasn't easy to hide the fact that something was wrong, though. Savannah's concentration was poor. She was preoccupied. And with a deep deficit in the lighthearted department, it was a struggle for her to contribute to Ivey's joy.

"Okay. Let's have it," Ivey finally said as they were getting ready for the seven-o'clock candlelight ceremony to be held at their cousin Jackson's house across the road.

Ivey's gown was an ankle-length white lace concoction with a tight bodice, a high neck, long knuckle-skimming sleeves and a skirt that flared from just below her hips downward. Savannah's dress was a similar but less extravagant design of dark purple velvet, cut in a long, lean A-line. Both gowns closed up the back with three dozen tiny covered buttons, and as they took turns fastening each other, Ivey seized the moment to question Savannah.

"Let's have what?" Savannah played dumb as she carefully eased the small buttons through the lace.

"You spent the night with Clint, walked home alone this morning from who-knows-where, and have been lost in space ever since. Deep, dark, ugly space, unless I miss my guess, because you look as if your dog died."

"We don't have a dog."

"You know what I mean. So let's have it."

"It's no big deal, Ivey. Not something that we need to talk about today of all days. This is an upbeat time for you. No downers."

"So you admit you're down."

It seemed fruitless to deny it at that point.

"Just tell me what's going on, will you?" Ivey persisted. "I'll worry a lot more if you leave me guessing than if you let me in on it."

Savannah thought about that. She put herself in Ivey's shoes and knew her sister was right. They'd been too close not to be tuned in to each other and not to worry about each other like two mother hens.

"Clint asked me to marry him," Savannah finally said after making her decision for her sister's sake if not her own. Then she went on to give Ivey the whole story, complete with most of what had gone through her mind and her reasons for turning him down.

"Oh, Savannah," Ivey groaned when Savannah had finished.

"You know how I feel," Savannah said defensively in answer to the disapproval and disappointment in her sister's tone.

"I know how you feel, all right. And I know what you're doing. It's you who doesn't see it for what it is."

That took Savannah by surprise. "I don't see what I'm doing for what it is, but you do?"

"Better than you do. I've watched you beat yourself up over losing that baby for fifteen years now. This is just the culmination of it."

"I'm not beating myself up over it."

"Of course you are. You've been punishing yourself all this time for letting Silas know you were pregnant, for not protecting the baby from him. Maybe for getting pregnant in the first place. I've seen you bury yourself in work rather than have a life, because you can't forgive yourself."

"You're wrong."

"I'm not wrong. You've always felt responsible for everything and everyone. And you've never gone easy on yourself if you've thought you didn't live up to those responsibilities. I knew even when you were in the thick of things with Clint fifteen years ago that you wouldn't stay here to be with him. I didn't have a doubt that you'd go through with our plans to leave home, because you'd see it as your responsibility to me. Of course you saw that pregnancy, that baby as your responsibility—''

"They *were* my responsibility."

"Okay, granted. But that fight with Silas wasn't."

"I should have gone to Clint with the news first. I shouldn't have breathed a word of it within fifty miles of Silas."

"Hindsight is twenty-twenty, Savannah. You thought he was out of earshot. You thought you *were* being careful. You didn't do anything to willfully cause what happened. And when it did there was nothing you could have done to stop it. You were trying to get away from him, remember? Trying to protect your baby. You were being responsible. Silas was just meaner and madder and bigger and quicker. There was nothing you could have done to prevent him from doing just what he did.

"But still you've spent the last fifteen years punishing yourself. And now you're punishing yourself more than ever by denying yourself what you want most. By denying yourself a happy future with Clint—the man you've loved since you were a teenager—as if you don't deserve to have him."

*Deserve.*

There *that* was again. And it was the one feeling she hadn't told Ivey about.

But before she could refute it, her sister continued. "You aren't giving that baby life by refusing to have one yourself, Savannah. By refusing happiness or love or a normal future and being a mother to other babies. That baby is lost, one way or another. And through no fault of your own—you're the only one who doesn't see that. But since you don't, then at least forgive yourself for it."

In the middle of things they'd switched positions so that they ended up with Ivey fastening Savannah's dress. But instead of stepping away now that she had, she grabbed Savannah by the shoulders from behind and gave her a little hug that only amounted to squeezing Savannah's shoulders and laying her chin lightly on one of them so as not to muss up what had been hours of preparation for the wedding.

"Don't forget that I was there," Ivey said. Then she reiterated, "It was Silas's doing. All of it. Not yours. And you've paid for it long enough. It's time to go on. Time to let yourself love again. Time to love *Clint* again."

It was also time to go to the wedding because Linc and Kansas pulled up the drive and stopped in front of the house to pick them up just then.

Still, Ivey didn't let go of her hold on Savannah.

"Give me that for a wedding gift," she said in a voice that sounded suddenly congested with tears. "Give me you forgiving yourself and going on. Give me you giving yourself a life as happy as I'm going to have with Cully. Please. There's nothing else I want."

Ivey and Cully's wedding was a very small affair in Jackson's living room. Only the Culhanes and Hellers attended, once more in deference to the recent death of Bucky Dennehy.

Savannah was Ivey's maid of honor and—as was

decided by the flip of a coin between Yance and Clint—Clint was Cully's best man.

Savannah didn't consider the outcome of that flipped coin to be a lucky one for her.

When the entrance music played to begin Savannah and Ivey's procession they were upstairs, out of sight. There were no lights on in the house or the stairway from which Savannah led the way down; the foyer and the living room were all illuminated only by white candles.

But even in the dimness, the moment she made the turn from the foot of the steps toward the living room where Clint stood beside the waiting Cully, Clint was the only person she was aware of.

Not that being in the same room with him would have been much less difficult for her. But walking toward him, stopping only two lengths away from him, standing before the minister as attendants in a wedding that wasn't their own, seemed to raise more feelings in her than she believed might have if he'd been merely a part of the onlookers.

It didn't help that Clint hardly looked at her beyond casting her a perfunctory nod when she first joined him and Cully. Or that when she hazarded a glance at him his expression was too blank to read and left her without any idea of what was going through his mind. Because *her* mind was still a jumble of troubled thoughts.

And voices repeating words that had been said to her since his proposal.

His words from that morning, Ivey's words from

just before the wedding, haunted her like distant music she couldn't stop listening to.

*People—especially kids—make mistakes. That doesn't mean you have to pay for it for the rest of your life....*

*You're punishing yourself by denying yourself what you want most...as if you don't deserve to have him....*

Was she punishing herself? she wondered, as the minister began to talk about weathering the sorrows of marriage as well as enjoying the pleasures.

She wasn't consciously punishing herself, no.

But she hadn't made much of a life for herself, either, she had to admit.

Sure, she'd gone to college, gotten her degrees, gone to work. But that was it. She worked. She didn't do anything that wasn't school related for fun—except an occasional dinner or movie with Ivey. She rarely dated. She rarely traveled. She didn't even have any hobbies.

She watched the people around her meet mates, marry, start families. She listened to them tell her about their vacations. Their weekends away. Their romantic trysts. Their plans to buy houses, broaden their horizons, invest in their dreams.

But she only sat on the sidelines of those kinds of things.

Being back in Elk Creek, seeing Clint, falling in love with him all over again, made that existence seem like exactly what Ivey had called it—denying herself a life. Punishing herself. Because even though she hadn't been unhappy in it, she hadn't been thrilled to get out of bed every morning, either, or looked forward to much of anything.

She'd basically just gone through the motions. Walked through each day without thinking about the bigger picture. The long run. The future. Without thinking about whether or not she was happy or fulfilled. Without dreading it, but also without dreaming.

But now she couldn't help looking toward the future, toward what lay ahead for her if she stayed on the path she'd set for herself.

She'd go back to Cheyenne. Alone. Without Ivey. She'd finish her thesis. Return to teaching.

She'd go on just the way she had for the past fifteen years—watching other people's lives from the sidelines.

But that didn't stand up too well in comparison to the idea of marrying Clint. Sharing a life with him. having a family....

Yet that idea still raised a whole slew of uncomfortable feelings in her.

And it suddenly occurred to her that those uncomfortable feelings were guilt. Guilt and the sense that she really didn't deserve Clint. Didn't deserve happiness. Didn't deserve a life when her child hadn't had the chance for one.

Realizing just how ingrained was that guilt, that sense of being undeserving, brought her up short.

The guilt had always been there but she hadn't recognized it in this form before. Of course she knew she felt guilty for even inadvertently letting her father know about the pregnancy when she had, for not protecting her baby from him.

But never before had she realized that she also felt guilty for her own life continuing when that child's hadn't. For being happy or finding joy in something when that child had never known a day of it.

But it was there now, in clear focus—guilt for having what her child had been denied. And the need to be punished for what she was guilty of.

Ivey had been right. In a way Savannah had been punishing herself all this time by denying herself what she really wanted. What she'd always wanted. What would make her genuinely happy. Clint.

His words rang through her mind again: *People— especially kids—make mistakes. That doesn't mean you have to pay for it for the rest of your life....*

What if, Savannah suddenly asked herself, one of her students came to her and said they'd made a mistake? The mistake of underestimating another person? Of underestimating what that person could overhear and what their reaction would be? And what if that underestimation had had dire consequences?

What would she say to that student?

It took her a moment to imagine someone other than herself in the scenario. To imagine herself as the counselor to a student standing in her shoes.

But when she managed that she couldn't see herself telling that student that he or she had to pay for the mistake forever. Not that they had to forfeit the rest of their life.

She'd say that the consequences were a tragedy. A terrible, terrible tragedy that had come from youthful misjudgment. That the student should learn what they could from it and go on...

So why had her sentence to herself been so much more stringent?

Except that her sister had been right about her tendency to be harder on herself than she would ever be on anyone else.

And it struck Savannah in that moment that something else Ivey had said was true. She wasn't giving life to the child she'd lost by denying herself. She wasn't changing the past. The baby was still gone one way or another...

That fact still had the power to torment her. To stab her like a knife.

But even so, she finally managed to acknowledge that maybe it *was* time she forgave herself for the mistake that had caused it.

Time she stopped punishing herself.

Because the longer she thought about it in this clearer light, with this new perspective, the more she realized there had been merit in what Clint and Ivey had said.

No, no one could convince her that she hadn't been responsible for that life she'd carried so long ago. Or for not being more careful about how she'd let her father find out about it.

But maybe the time really had come to put it behind her. To go on. Maybe she had earned a little happiness after fifteen years of punishing herself.

On the other hand, that was easier to decide than to feel.

But as she stood before the minister, by her sister's side, Savannah worked hard at it.

She had to.

Because Clint was only a few feet away.

The Culhane brothers had purchased new suits for the occasion—not Western-cut suits but well-tailored business suits that didn't give them away as the cowboys they were, had it not been for their boots. They all looked incredibly handsome in them, but it was only Clint who Savannah couldn't stop looking at.

Clint who made her heart swell with love.

That love didn't keep her from remembering the child they'd lost, she told herself. It wouldn't lessen the weight of what had happened.

But standing there before the minister with him, she finally came to accept that she did deserve to love him and be loved by him. That she did deserve a life with him even if she had made a very big mistake a long time ago. That not to give in to the love they shared would be another mistake that only made the first one a bigger tragedy. It was a risk, but one she needed to take.

"I now pronounce you man and wife."

The minister's voice rose louder than it had been during the ceremony, yanking Savannah out of her thoughts.

*Man and wife.*

She and Clint.

But everyone was gathering around Ivey and Cully to congratulate them by then, and Savannah had to remind herself that this was her sister's day. That she couldn't rush into Clint's arms at that same moment and tell him she'd changed her mind. That she loved him. That she wanted to marry him.

Besides, he was acting the way he had on those

first few occasions they'd found themselves together
again when she'd come back to Elk Creek—removed,
remote, as aloof as if they were merely two strangers
who happened to have mutual acquaintances.

*Maybe I blew it,* she thought. *Maybe it's too late
and I've ruined things once and for all.*

But for the moment she couldn't explore the possibilities. She could only put a smile on her face, hug
her sister and new brother-in-law, wait for a better
opportunity to approach Clint.

And hope for the best....

The table in Jackson and Ally's dining room was
large enough to seat everyone at once, so an elaborate
wedding supper was served—also by candlelight.
Ally had done the cooking and food preparation, and
they'd hired several high school students to serve and
do the cleanup so none of the guests had to be taken
away from the celebration.

They dined on salads of butter lettuce dressed with
a delicate raspberry vinaigrette, crab mousse, vichys-
soise, prime rib of beef, steamed asparagus, tiny new
potatoes in a garlic-herb-butter sauce and crisp French
bread. Champagne flowed freely, and toasts and
funny stories were the order of the day as conversation included the entire table rather than small fac-
tions breaking off to talk privately.

It made the meal easier for Savannah because she
didn't have to contribute much more than laughter at
what was being said. That was a good thing, because
her brain wasn't firing on all burners. The only thing
she could really think about was Clint, when she

might be able to talk to him, and what his response would be.

He seemed to be enjoying himself. He toasted the newlyweds twice. He told an amusing story about Cully's first kiss. He laughed with the rest of them when someone else relayed an anecdote.

But Savannah thought his gaiety seemed slightly forced.

Or maybe she only hoped it was. Because hers was. And maybe if his was, too, that meant he was as unhappy to be apart from her as she was to be apart from him.

But she worried a little that his forced gaiety—if she wasn't imagining that it was forced—came instead from the fact that he just didn't like having to be in the same room with her. Especially since he rarely glanced in her direction, he never spoke directly to her, and he could well have been trying to completely ignore her existence altogether.

Unfortunately Savannah couldn't ignore his.

He was nearer the head of the table than she was. Which caused him to be in her line of vision as each toast, each story was aimed at Ivey and Cully. So she couldn't help looking at him time and again.

If he was upset by the events of the morning and her turning down his proposal it didn't show as strain in his face. He was as ruggedly handsome as ever. His hair had been more meticulously combed than usual for the ceremony, but the moment it was over he seemed to have relaxed into his normally less-formal attitude. He'd run his fingers through his hair once or twice so it had that roughed-up appearance

that was so appealing. He, along with most of the rest
of the men in the group, had loosened his tie and
opened his collar button. He'd also shed his jacket
and rolled the cuffs of his dress shirt to just below
his elbows.

It all suited him better than the more trussed-up
appearance, and nearly made Savannah's mouth water
with each glance.

The meal went on and on—or at least that's how
it seemed to her—before the wedding cake was cut
and served.

Then Ivey went upstairs to change clothes so she
and Cully could head for Cheyenne, from where they
were set to leave the next morning on their honeymoon in the Bahamas.

On her way back down the stairs Ivey called Savannah's name, and when Savannah turned from
where everyone was standing in the living room
again, Ivey tossed her the bouquet.

Savannah caught the flying flowers reflexively.
And just as reflexively—and for no reason she had
thought out ahead of time—tossed it to Clint.

That started an uproar of levity, jokes and teasing,
but Savannah was less aware of that than of Clint.
Her eyes locked with his, and his brows did a confused dip even as he went along with the merriment
of the moment.

Then Ivey and Cully said their goodbyes and ran
to Cully's truck amid a shower of rice that rained
down upon them as everyone followed them out into
the courtyard and all the way to the drive.

Cully started the engine and drove off with a loud

horn honking and a wave, and that was that. Cully and Ivey were married, and the party to celebrate it moved inside once more, lured by Jackson's offer of nightcaps.

But as Savannah began to head toward the house with everyone else she felt a familiar hand on her arm, keeping her from going in with the group.

Clint didn't say anything as he held her there, and no one seemed to notice that they were hanging back. But as Savannah watched them all go she discovered that as anxious as she'd been to be alone with Clint so she could try to rescind her rejection of his proposal, she was suddenly just that nervous about facing him.

"Brrr...it's cold out here," she said, alluding to their going into the warmth of the house, too.

But Clint paid no attention to that allusion. Instead, once the rest of the wedding guests were out of earshot, he said, "So what was that bouquet business about?"

Savannah's cold feet weren't coming from the cobbled courtyard floor they were standing on. "Would you believe it slipped out of my hands?" she hedged with a joke.

But Clint was frowning down at her and no longer looked to be in a joking mood.

"Talk to me, Savannah," he ordered.

"We'll freeze to death."

"Okay," he said as if accepting a feeble challenge.

His hand slipped down her arm to take her hand and pull her to where his truck was parked in the circular drive in front of the house. He went around to the driver's side, opened the door, nearly lifted her onto the seat and climbed in after her. Then he turned on the engine, put it into gear with more force than it required and left stones shooting out behind them as he sped down the drive from Jackson's place, crossed the road and stopped only inches short of Savannah's porch.

There, he flung the door open again, hopped down without fanfare, reached back in to slide her out with him, slammed the door and ushered her into her own house.

It was only after he'd done all that that he stalled.

In her entryway. At the foot of the stairs she'd fallen down fifteen years before.

He scowled at them as darkly as if he'd come face-to-face with evil, and Savannah didn't have to be told what he was thinking about.

But after a moment he drew himself up, spun on his heels to look at her and said, "Now. Talk to me."

And she did.

It wasn't easy at first to tell him all she'd thought about since they'd parted that morning. All she'd finally come to see. All she'd finally put into perspective.

But the longer she explained things that were new even to her, the more she warmed up—literally and figuratively.

It didn't hurt to have Clint's eyes on her the whole time, to watch them go from cold, hard and angry, to gradually relaxed, soft, loving again.

"I won't ever be able to stop ruing that day or what happened," she said as she finished filling him in.

"But I think you and Ivey are both right about me forgiving myself for the mistake, putting it behind me, going on."

"This better not be a roundabout way of telling me you're leaving for Cheyenne."

"Actually it's a roundabout way of telling you I'd like not to leave."

"Could you find a roundabout way of telling me you'll marry me?"

Relief flooded through her at last and let her smile the first honest-to-goodness smile she'd had all evening.

"It wouldn't be okay if I just said, Yes, I'll marry you—straight out?"

"Yeah, that would probably be okay."

He didn't budge from where he was standing beside the staircase, looking across to where Savannah stood in the archway between the foyer and the living room.

And Savannah expected him to move. She expected him to close the gap, to take her in his arms, to kiss her, to tell her he loved her.

But still he just stood there, studying her. Waiting.

Then he shook his head in mock disgust, rolled those incredible crystal blue eyes, shifted his weight to one leg and put both hands on his hips. "So say it."

"Say it?"

"Say, yes, I'll marry you."

Ah. He was teasing her.

Well, she could give as good as she got. "I haven't heard the question to go with it yet."

He gave her a slow-spreading grin that deepened the creases in his cheeks. "Want me down on one knee?"

"No, standing in place will do fine," she said, sounding very much the schoolteacher.

Clint finally stepped in front of her and took her right hand in both of his much bigger, more powerful ones.

But still he didn't propose.

He did that nonchalant weight shift again, looked to the ceiling and shook his head once more as if asking divine forbearance for their silliness.

Then he captured her eyes with his, smiled more sweetly and said, "Savannah Heller, will you be my wife?"

She cocked her head and looked at the ceiling out of the corner of her eye as if seeking permission from whatever spirits he'd been consulting before. Then she looked back at Clint, struck anew by how gorgeous he was.

"Yes, Clint Culhane, I'll marry you."

"Finally," he breathed, as if he'd thought this moment might never come.

He pulled her into his arms and held her that way for a little while as he breathed a relieved sigh into her hair.

Then he eased his grip enough to look down at her.

"I love you, lady."

"I love you, too."

His mouth sealed that declaration with a kiss that was initially as tender and tentative as if he thought he might be having a dream and that too firm a buss might awaken him.

But it didn't stay that way for long before his lips parted over hers, urging hers to do the same and sending a mischievous tongue to court her.

Yet even that deeper kiss was all too brief. He ended it to enfold her in a tight hug that seemed to fulfill a need in Clint to have her so close against him it was as if he were trying to absorb her into his skin.

"Think if we went back across the road we could get the minister to marry us now?"

"No. You know we need blood tests and a license."

"I've waited long enough for you. I don't want to wait anymore. How about we drive into the city, catch a plane for Las Vegas and do it there?"

Savannah made a face against his chest. "How about we do the red tape stuff and wait just until Ivey and Cully get home, so they can be with us?"

"A week? You keep me waitin' fifteen years and now you want another week?"

"I'll make it go so fast you won't even notice."

He reared back just enough to look down at her. "Yeah?" he said, sounding intrigued. "How will you do that?"

"I'll figure something out," she promised with a voice full of innuendo.

"Okay. A week. But not a day more. It's been long enough, you know."

"I know," she whispered.

Clint lowered his head to kiss her again. More passionately now. More sensually.

Savannah met and matched him, savoring the feel of his body wrapped around hers, his strong arms enfolding her, the feel of his mouth on hers, his tongue dancing and playing and rejoicing with hers.

She loved this man. More than she'd ever let herself acknowledge before.

And she could wait a week to marry him.

But only a week.

Because it was time for them to start the life they should have begun all those years ago. Time to rid herself of all her fears. Time to finally be together the way she truly believed they were meant to be.

And if they were fifteen years late?

There was only one thing she could say to that.

Better late than never.

Much, much better late than never.

\*     \*     \*     \*     \*

# Return to the Towers!

### In March
*New York Times* bestselling author

# NORA ROBERTS

brings us to the Calhouns' fabulous
Maine coast mansion and reveals the
tragic secrets hidden there for generations.

For all his degrees, Professor Max Quartermain has a
lot to learn about love—and luscious Lilah Calhoun is
just the woman to teach him. Ex-cop Holt Bradford is
as prickly as a thornbush—until Suzanna Calhoun's
special touch makes love blossom in his heart.
And all of them are caught in the race to solve
the generations-old mystery of a priceless
lost necklace…and a timeless love.

# *Lilah and Suzanna*
## THE
## Calhoun Women

### A special 2-in-1 edition containing
### FOR THE LOVE OF LILAH and
### SUZANNA'S SURRENDER

Available at your favorite retail outlet.

## RETURN TO WHITEHORN

Silhouette's beloved **MONTANA MAVERICKS** returns with brand-new stories from your favorite authors! Welcome back to Whitehorn, Montana—a place where rich tales of passion and adventure are unfolding under the Big Sky. The new generation of Mavericks will leave you breathless!

### Coming from Silhouette Special Edition®:

**February 98: LETTER TO A LONESOME COWBOY by Jackie Merritt**

**March 98: WIFE MOST WANTED by Joan Elliott Pickart**

**May 98: A FATHER'S VOW by Myrna Temte**

**June 98: A HERO'S HOMECOMING by Laurie Paige**

### And don't miss these two very special additions to the Montana Mavericks saga:

MONTANA MAVERICKS WEDDINGS
by Diana Palmer, Ann Major and Susan Mallery
Short story collection available April 98

WILD WEST WIFE by Susan Mallery
Harlequin Historicals available July 98

Round up these great new stories
at your favorite retail outlet.

## ALICIA SCOTT

**Continues the twelve-book series—36 Hours—in March 1998 with Book Nine**

# PARTNERS IN CRIME

The storm was over, and Detective Jack Stryker finally had a prime suspect in Grand Springs' high-profile murder case. But beautiful Josie Reynolds wasn't about to admit to the crime—nor did Jack want her to. He believed in her innocence, and he teamed up with the alluring suspect to prove it. But was he playing it by the book—or merely blinded by love?

For Jack and Josie and *all* the residents of Grand Springs, Colorado, the storm-induced blackout was just the beginning of 36 Hours that changed *everything!* You won't want to miss a single book.

Available at your favorite retail outlet.

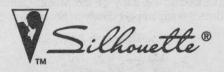

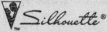